The Outcasts

By the Author

Steel and Promise

The Outcasts

The Outcasts

by

Alexa Black

2018

THE OUTCASTS

ISBN 13: 978-1-63555-242-3

This Trade Paperback Original Is Published By
Bold Strokes Books, Inc.
P.O. Box 249
Valley Falls, NY 12185

First Edition: July 2018

Credits
Editor: Cindy Cresap
Production Design: Susan Ramundo
Cover Design By Sheri (hindsightgraphics@gmail.com)

Acknowledgments

Thanks to everyone who gave me feedback and ideas, and thanks especially to Theo and Kat for such thorough beta reading. You're still both wonderful, both at encouraging me and at letting me know when I need to fix something.

Thanks to Cindy, my editor. Thanks to Sandy for the conversation that led to this book. And, as always, thanks to the rest of the BSB team. Getting to know so many of you has been wonderful.

Dedication

To Kat D and Theo T, for sticking with me and my stories.

Chapter One

This wasn't her shuttle.

Bluish light flooded Sue's vision, far brighter than the light in her little craft. It stung her eyes, and everything looked blurry anyway. She closed her eyes again.

She was lying down, on something less than comfortable. Her bad leg ached, and she frowned. Had she injured it again somehow? Had she crashed?

This couldn't be her shuttle. She would feel it moving under her.

I must be on a planet. I must have made it.

But where?

She remembered light and sound. One moment she'd been looking at the stars, studying, searching. Cursing herself for a fool. *You're just a spacebus driver. You'll never find anything new out here. You haven't even been to the outer colonies.*

The next moment the sky had opened up, a jagged lightning streak across the star-spangled black, and she couldn't have pulled away even if she'd wanted to.

"Well, you found something," she tried to say. It came out as a weak moan.

She cracked her eyes open again. The cold light stung, but this time she knew it was coming.

A figure hovered over her, its silhouette dark against the light. Or was it really that color? Aliens could look like anything. She squinted.

More light, in the wrong places. Streaks of it, across the creature's figure, as if it made its own light.

"You are awake," said a voice, deep and echoing and clearly not human.

She rubbed her eyes. "Yes, I'm awake." Well, at least she could talk now. "Where am I?"

She bit her lip to keep from saying "What are you?" She'd found someone. An alien. She'd gone exploring and found aliens. That was better than whatever she'd hoped for, and she wanted to know everything.

But she couldn't just demand they tell her all about themselves, as if they existed just for her to find them. That seemed rude.

But she did look at the creature. The woman, she corrected herself.

The alien woman would have towered over Sue even if she hadn't been lying on some strange cot. But she was muscular too, broad-framed like an athlete. Or a soldier. Did these aliens like strangers?

Sue didn't know yet. But this one wasn't threatening. That was a start. Athlete, then. Hadn't athletes competed naked, somewhere in the far-off history of Earth?

Well, this alien looked like that. Right down to the naked.

She looked enough like a human woman that Sue couldn't help but stare. She blinked, trying to clear her head again.

She'd been right. She hadn't just seen a dark shape against the light. The woman's skin wasn't black but gray, a deep, rich charcoal. The warmer light she'd seen came from the woman's body too, bright glowing streaks of light crossing her body, almost like molten cracks in stone. One tore across the right side of her chin, like an illuminated scar.

Sue stared at them. Some kind of bioluminescence, she guessed. But she couldn't help but wonder just what was under this creature's skin.

Something shimmered around the alien's body, as if the light of the room had shifted. Shadows settled around her shoulders. Was that just this room, or just that Sue was groggy, or something else? Parts of the alien gave off light. Could parts of her also…give off darkness? It looked that way to Sue. The shadows followed her visitor around. Moved when she moved.

That was too weird to reason out right now, and staring still hurt Sue's eyes, so she looked up at the alien's face again. Her eyes were the same color as her scars, a fiery yellow. They gleamed, like the scars did. The alien had a long face, with sculpted cheekbones. Not just high, but like someone had carved them out of rock. Or whatever this woman's skin was made of.

She had horns on her head, two of them, curling up from her forehead.

Those looked familiar. Too familiar. Like something out of a story. *Aliens should look weirder than that. Especially aliens from out past the Rim.*

"Drink this," the alien said. Her teeth were sharp, and Sue caught a glimpse of gold when her lips moved. Did the inside of her mouth glow too?

Nothing else. No answer to Sue's question about where the hell this planet was. Not even a greeting.

Well, Sue had forgotten hello too. So she couldn't hold it against her hostess.

And that wasn't the only strange thing.

Sue looked down at the alien's hands. She held out a black bowl. The liquid inside glowed, a cool blue that matched the light of the room.

Sue reached out for it. It felt cool to the touch.

Pure curiosity made her press it to her lips. It smelled bracing, like mint.

She stopped just before she opened her mouth. Did aliens even know what humans ate?

"I don't know what this is." Sue looked down, apologetic.

"It will nourish you," the alien replied.

Sue watched her lips move, saw that gold shimmer again when she opened her mouth. *What the hell are you made of?*

But the alien was waiting for her to try the—drink? Soup? Her hand twitched with impatience, and Sue saw that her fingers ended in sharp claws.

"Bottoms up," she muttered. She'd gone looking for aliens, and now she'd found them. And this one was trying to take care of her. Whatever that meant, it was better than several alternatives.

She might as well see where this would take her.

The liquid tasted like she'd expected, cool and minty. A tingling spread through her sore leg, a pleasant chill that numbed its ache.

She took another careful sip. If this was meant to kill the pain, did the alien know how much of it a human needed?

The cool feeling changed, as though the liquid were warming in her mouth or in her body. The chill became a faint heat, and her tight muscles began to relax.

The alien smiled. Or smirked. Sue couldn't tell quite well enough to read her body language.

"Thank you." Sue tipped the last of the liquid into her mouth. The warm feeling grew, a bright fire under her skin. Intense enough to be distracting, especially with a naked alien standing right in front of her. It felt almost like desire, and Sue blinked to keep herself from staring.

If the alien noticed, she didn't let on. "Now. What is your name?"

Well, if the alien wanted Sue's name, maybe she'd tell Sue hers. "Just my name? Not where I'm from?"

"I know where humans come from."

Oh, you do? Good, because I have no idea where I am right now. "Sue Jones."

She offered her hand to shake. If the alien knew about humans, she might know about that. And looked a lot like a human, at least for the moment. Maybe they had some other things in common, too.

The alien didn't take her hand. She nodded instead. "Kara."

"Well, thank you, Kara. This"—she tilted her head at the empty bowl—"is it medicine, or food?"

"You are not seriously injured."

"Okay. Food, then. This food was great. It really helped."

"But it should also ease whatever pain you might feel."

"Yeah. Yeah, it did. Thanks."

Kara didn't answer that. She just stared down at Sue. The shadows danced around her again, a little swirl just past her back.

That's not the lights in this room, is it?

She looked around. The room was plain, as was the cot she lay on. But behind her stood a flat computer screen, readings scrolling across it in blue glyphs Sue didn't recognize. A wavy line appeared and disappeared. A graph of her vitals?

That would make this a medical room of some kind. Which would make sense, after a crash. But what about this alien? Was she something like a nurse, or just especially nice to alien visitors who got stuck in storms that might be wormholes?

Sue chewed her lip and stared at the golden lines running over Kara's body. Even if these aliens went everywhere naked, she doubted that doctors and nurses would be so casual about treating aliens.

Unless they knew humans well enough to know they weren't a danger.

She looked at Kara; Kara looked at her. Neither spoke.

Sue swallowed hard. If she wanted to know, she'd have to ask. "Where am I?"

"The Ring. Around the World of Flame."

"What? Where is that? I don't understand. My ship was—"

"Caught, yes. And brought here."

"Right. But where is here?"

Kara's lips closed. No hint of light shone through them.

"Please. I appreciate you taking care of me. And I'd love to look around a while, now that I'm here." Was that too forward? Maybe it was. But she'd zoomed off in an unauthorized shuttle to get here, after all.

The shadows around Kara swirled again, and her eyes glowed a bright yellow. "You should rest."

Sue sighed. She'd found the aliens, and all they wanted her to do was lie down? "I'm sure you're right. But I need to know where I am, so I can eventually get home."

Kara looked at her for a long moment. That little smirky smile disappeared, and Sue shivered. Kara had looked stern before, and she hadn't exactly been friendly. But she'd looked like she was trying to help, at least.

This was different. *That was the wrong question, wasn't it?*

"I do not know," Kara said and turned away.

Sue saw a flare of shadow over Kara's back, and through it the glow of two massive scars.

What are you?

Chapter Two

Sue looked around her little room. It was plain, with smooth white walls, blue light shining from fixtures on the ceiling and walls. She had her small cot to lie on, a mirror across from it, a small cabinet where she could put her few possessions. Glyphs scrolled across a screen behind it, but Sue couldn't tell if it was a videoscreen with channels she hadn't figured out how to change, or a hospital room's record of her own vitals, or both. A small stall had been cut into one corner of the room, with a toilet and a space to shower.

But nowhere to wash her laundry. She'd have to ask about that, that and clothes to wear. She didn't feel terribly dirty yet, not when she'd just gotten to some strange alien world. But one shirt and pair of pants—and one set of underwear—would get dirty fast. And she didn't think the aliens wore clothes.

Which was a bit awkward. But there wasn't much she could do about it for the moment.

And whoever her benefactor had been, Kara seemed to be the only alien who bothered with humans. She'd called out to some of them. They'd turned their horned heads, looked at her a moment, and stalked off like she'd insulted them.

And even Kara had been cold. She hadn't introduced herself, not right away. Just made sure Sue was drinking her juice or whatever it was, and only introduced herself after long moments.

You're not like the others, are you?

Too many mysteries. Sue pulled out her small tablet and turned it on. She doubted it would receive anything from home. She didn't even know how far away the colonies were, much less how far they could transmit data.

And it was stormy tonight. Today? Whichever. Sue could hear the rumble of thunder outside somewhere. Even if she wasn't far away, that could mean she wouldn't get a signal either.

Pointless, then. But there were riots going on back in her colony. She closed her eyes and could see the fire, scorched on the back of her eyelids. What was happening back home?

She exhaled hard. She'd stolen the damn shuttle to get away from the flames and the fighting. And it felt good to be here, in a pristine little room, cleaner than Sue had been in years. Drinking strange alien soup that nourished her better than the swill at home. Curling up on a cot that didn't have any holes.

It was almost a relief to be bored.

Almost. She blinked down at the tablet.

Images and glyphs appeared on the screen, but when she tapped her fingers to them, nothing happened. Error messages blinked, filling the display, generic little messages about not finding any signals.

Yeah. Don't vanish through random wormholes. Sue shrugged and tossed the device onto a little table near her cot, more forcefully than she meant to.

Kara had taken the shadows with her. The room was even duller now, the lights searingly bright, with no swirl of light and shade. How had Kara done that?

She'd caught a glimpse of an answer when Kara walked away. Those scars on her back, between her shoulder blades. Golden gouges deep in them, like the lines on her skin.

But too big, too thick. Not like her bright streaks. Lumpy and misshapen, the light in them pulsing too slowly. They looked like they hurt. Or like they had hurt, a long time ago.

And the shadows had curled around her from there.

Sue shuddered. Did that mean all of Kara's streaks were scars?

She curled up on the alien cot and tried to sleep.

❖

"Come with me."

Sue blinked. *Come with you? It took you forever to get to your name.*

This time her vision cleared right away. Either she felt better, or that blue stuff was impressive.

But she found herself staring at Kara's chest, at the rough stony texture, the light inside the scars. She hurried to sit up and look anywhere else. Being rude right when Kara had offered something like that would be a disaster.

"You wished to see our world, did you not?"

Sue sprang up, forgetting the ache in her leg. This was too good to be true. "Yes!"

"Then come."

Sue patted down her clothes and tried her best to smooth out wrinkles in the fabric. She hadn't showered yet, just poked at her tablet and slept, and these aliens all looked so clean. Did they even get dirty?

Compared to them, she would've been a mess even if she had managed a shower.

Hi, I'm Sue. A sweaty short little human with a bum leg who got lost and still isn't quite sure how. Glad to make your acquaintance. So what do you think of our species so far?

Kara, for her part, still wasn't saying much. She just walked ahead of Sue with precise, measured strides, too long for Sue to keep up easily.

Especially with the leg. The miracle meals helped, whatever they were. But pain happened sometimes, especially after you'd been reconstructed. The doctors were good at what they did, but they weren't Mother Nature. Especially if you were destined to be something like a spacebus driver.

Sue bit her lip and fought to keep up. She'd wanted to be a starfighter pilot once. Before she'd realized the military took people who hadn't needed rearranging to move right. Once she had realized it, she'd almost gone crazy. If she was just going to sit in a cockpit most of the time anyway, what did she need a perfect leg for?

Kara led her into a narrow little hall. All around them rose glass windows, slanting from the floor to a high ceiling. Sue rushed to one, eager to see anything at all.

There wasn't much nearby. Just other corridors, like this one, with a few taller towers that looked like the building she'd just come out of.

But beyond them stood high halls, tubes that gleamed with light. People who passed in and out of them, talking and laughing. Their voices sounded hollow, like Kara's, but they didn't seem solemn. Others inside greeted them. She couldn't tell what anyone was saying, but she stretched out a hand, like a curious child.

So many people. People like Kara.

All of them were taller than humans, and they all had gray skin, but they weren't all as dark as Kara. Just like human skin color went from pink to brown, theirs seemed to go from ghostly white to slate gray to obsidian black. A few were pale like ash.

Or marble, Sue thought, and wondered why she kept thinking of Earth rocks and stones. Wherever this was, they were a long way from the colonies and a longer way from Earth.

She looked back at the aliens. They all had the bright streaks, too, from yellows like Kara's to fiery orange to molten-metal red.

All of them had horns and claws, and all of them had two lines on their backs, just between their shoulders. Little bumps there, too, jagged bits of—what was it exactly? Stone? Skin?

Seeing them made Sue's fingers itch. Especially the one on Kara. If only she could touch that scar, soothe it with her fingers.

But none of the aliens seemed to notice their scars, or act like they hurt. And all of them moved amid clouds of shadow, like Kara did.

Just something about alien anatomy, then. Both the scars and the weird tricks of the light when they passed by. Sue bit her lip and stilled her twitching fingers. She'd wanted a mystery and now she had one. You didn't solve them overnight.

Sue tried to catch someone's eye, a slate-skinned man with bright red eyes. He looked at her a moment, those crimson eyes widening. Then his lip curled. He shook his head and moved away from the window.

She heard Kara's footfalls behind her and gritted her teeth. Kara had helped her, had done what she could to nurse her back to health. But Kara had also been cold.

Sue didn't need her comfort. Not for this. Not just because some alien guy didn't feel like saying hello.

She looked down, past the little bridges. Below lay red mist and clouds.

Angry ones. She could see whirling sand and purplish flares that looked like lightning. Was that a rainstorm or a whirlwind or both at once?

World of Flame, Kara had said. Was that coming next? "Is your weather always like this?"

A smile quirked Kara's lip. Sue could see the faint hint of the yellow light inside Kara's mouth.

That made her wonder all over again. Was there fire somewhere deep within the stone, like magma under rock?

How would it feel to kiss an alien?

"Our weather," Kara said like nothing had happened at all. Sue fought down a shudder and wished she weren't wearing such dirty clothes.

"Yeah. There's a storm. Like the one I got caught in, maybe. Back on the colonies, where I come from, there's not always… lightning like this. Not when it's dry."

Kara's expression softened. "We are outcasts."

Sue looked at Kara, then back at the window. She thought about the scar on Kara's back. "The planet, down below—"

"This is one of the Rings. Where we live. Down below is the World of Flame, like I told you yesterday." She looked down and her lip curled.

Sue squinted at the angry clouds. That didn't sound good. "Can anyone…uh…does anyone live down there?"

Kara tilted her head. "Live? Not exactly." Her frown deepened.

I'm asking the wrong questions.

The space beneath the bridge flared with light bright enough to hurt Sue's eyes.

"So you and the others I've seen, you live up here?"

"The outcasts? Yes. This—this planet, you would call it—is where we were sent. Where we were banished, in our exile." The streaks on Kara's skin flared with light, and Sue thought she saw her tremble.

Sue looked down again, then up at the bridge across from hers. "You were exiled and sent here." To a world full of storms, and lightning, and wind.

Kara nodded. "Yes."

"But up here it's all full of bridges. You have shelter."

"Everything we have, we built for ourselves. We were meant to live down there." Kara looked down. At her side, her clawed hands tightened into fists.

"Meant to live down there." Sue bit her lip. Even tall rock people with fire for innards would have a hard time living down there. And from Kara's stiff posture, Sue guessed Kara had tried.

How long ago had that been? And why would something like that happen?

She slid closer to Kara, reached out a hand, and laid it on her shoulder. The skin was hard, like stone, but warm and inviting.

Kara twitched under Sue's hand. Sue didn't move it. Kara needed comfort.

And Sue needed to ask. "Who sent you?"

Kara's eyes widened. Sue couldn't tell if Kara was looking at her or not. The glow in her eyes made it hard to tell. But Sue didn't think so. She didn't think Kara was looking at anything at all. Her lips twisted into a snarl and the light in her mouth brightened.

Wrong question, again. Sue let go of Kara's shoulder and backed away as best she could.

But Sue was a human with a bad leg on a strange world she didn't know yet. Kara was a native, and an athletic one. Her claws snagged the fabric of Sue's shirt. One pricked the skin beneath, and Sue bit her lip on a scream.

Kara blinked. She pulled her claws free from the fabric and her eyes narrowed again. She shook her head as if to clear it.

Sue stared down at the ragged tear. "You just attacked me!"

"Human."

Sue closed her mouth, looked over at Kara's claws, and shuddered. She edged backward along the bridge. What had she said? And more important than that, what would Kara do to her? She wouldn't be able to get away for long.

And of the aliens Sue had met so far, Kara was the friendliest.

"Sue," Kara tried. But her voice was no softer, and the shadows around her danced, like phantoms from some story.

Sue raised her head. If Kara caught up to her and wanted to do something...well. She'd wanted to be a soldier once. The least she could do was act like one. "I've done nothing to you!"

Kara's hand twitched, the claws curling. Sue let out a long, slow breath.

Kara lowered her hand and bowed her head. Sue stared at the horns. Were those a weapon too?

"You're right," Kara said at last. "You have done nothing."

She turned away, and Sue saw the scar again.

"They did that to you, didn't they?"

"What?"

Sue snapped her mouth shut. "Nothing."

CHAPTER THREE

"I need to clean myself. I need to clean these clothes."

And find some new ones. Sue looked down at her torn shirt. She looked bad enough next to these beautiful aliens. They were tall. She was short. They were elegant, the kind of beings who could pull off walking around naked everywhere. Sue was a mess in wrinkled clothes. *Is that why they reject me? Because next to them, I look like a damn fool?*

Kara tilted her head at Sue.

Sue raised her hands in exasperation. Kara was the last person she wanted to talk to right now. But she wasn't sure she had a choice. She could rush off toward one of the others and hope he'd take her in, but what if he lashed out at her like Kara had? And didn't miss?

Besides, Sue wasn't convinced Kara meant it. She still felt weird about it, yeah. A little scared, to be honest. Kara was an alien, a tall one with fangs and claws who looked big and strong for her kind. But where would Sue go if she ran now? Kara had cared when a tiny, fleshy little alien who didn't even know what the Rings were needed help. Would any of the rest of these creatures have done that?

And Kara had gone all weird, gone away, like people who'd been at the riots sometimes did when they remembered getting beaten. Sue had seen that before. Sue had—

She stopped herself. That wasn't good to think about. Not right now.

She willed herself to focus on Kara again. Kara's voice, low and echoing, asking if she was okay when she awoke. Kara's strange flesh, warm under her hand.

She bit her lip, just once, and forced herself to speak again. "Look, Kara. Just tell me. Is there anywhere I can wash these clothes?"

"Our kind don't use cloths often. But there is a place they can be cleaned, across the next bridge."

Sue smiled. "That's good. I'm feeling better. I'll go in a little bit."

Kara held out a hand. "Give them to me, then."

Sue looked at Kara's hand, then up at her face. Was she smirking? Sue couldn't tell.

"Give them to you? You mean right now?"

"You wanted them cleaned."

"Well, yes, but—" Sue's cheeks flushed. "I can't just take them off right now."

"Why?"

Sue looked down. "Because humans don't just get naked."

Kara looked blankly at her.

"I mean, don't just take off our clothes. The cloths we wear. Doing that means something."

Her cheeks burned. *Kara said she knows where humans come from. What if Kara wants to see you?*

She bit her lip to keep herself from blurting the thought out. Kara was gorgeous. Kara wouldn't want to stare at some sweaty little spacebus driver who hadn't even showered yet.

Hell, Kara was an alien. What would she want with a human in the first place?

Besides, knowing Sue's luck and the law of probability, Kara liked alien boys, anyway.

Kara was still looking at her. Great.

"What does it mean, Sue? Are you ashamed?"

"Ashamed?" Sue's head snapped up. That stung. Even though "ashamed" wasn't all that far from "embarrassed," and in front of these gorgeous aliens, embarrassed pretty much described it.

"Humans wear cloth because they are ashamed of their nakedness," Kara said.

"What? Where did you get that?"

"Everyone here knows that."

Sue's embarrassment curdled into anger. Everyone? Everyone who'd gawked at her and turned away in disgust? That everyone?

"You don't know shit about humans."

Pulling off her shoes and socks was the easy part.

She reached down, unzipped her pants, and pulled them down with a fierce, fluid motion before she could bother to regret it. Then she slipped off her torn shirt and stood in front of Kara in her underwear.

The shadows around Kara curled. Was it just Sue's imagination, or were her bioluminescent bits glowing a little brighter?

And she wasn't blinking. But Sue hadn't seen her blink much before either.

You got yourself into this. Sue stared straight at Kara and found the fastener of her bra behind her back. *So finish it.*

She let the bra fall and wrapped her fingers around the band of her underwear. She swallowed hard for courage, yanked them down, and stepped out of them.

Kara stared. Still not blinking. Did the aliens blink? Sue had noticed that they didn't do it much. But had they done it at all, or had she just assumed they would? Was Kara just looking, or was Kara staring as hard as Sue thought she was?

"So this is me," Sue said. "Not ashamed."

"No." Kara's lip twitched in what Sue had begun to recognize as the beginning of a smile. "You're not."

"Gonna admit now that you don't know as much about us as you thought?"

Kara laughed, the echoes softer than Sue had heard before. It made something thrill in her belly. Was Kara really puzzled by clothes, or had she wanted this?

"I do admit it," Kara said. "We've seen humans, but that doesn't mean we know them. Other than what old stories tell. Old stories about ancient humans that none of us would remember anyway. Except one."

"Except one?"

"The first of us is very old. He was there at the beginning of the world."

Sue blinked. "At the beginning of what world? There are lots of worlds out there." She waved a hand, indicating space.

Kara nodded. "There are. But there are more to worlds than you think, little human."

"What the hell is that supposed to mean?"

Kara's eyes flickered. Her smile disappeared. "Do you think you got here just because you flew for a long distance?"

"No. I got caught in a…" A wormhole. But who was she kidding? She didn't even know what those were. Not like a real pilot would. Just well enough to steer clear of weird looking bends in space when she flew her bus.

"In something," she finished, flushing again.

"There are beginnings and endings, and no one knows them all."

"But 'the first' did? I—if I wasn't talking to someone who knew more about this world than me, I'd say that sounds more like religion than facts."

Kara's lip twisted and Sue winced. Maybe Sue really had offended her.

Kara gave her a wry smile. "Yes. I suppose it does." She glanced over at the pile of clothes. "Do you want me to take that for you?"

"Now?"

"So that you can clean yourself in peace."

Sue chuckled. *So now that I've already got the sexy alien looking at me, she decides to respect my privacy?*

Perfect.

But asking her to stay would be making a confession.

"All right," Sue said.

"Very well." Kara bowed and picked up the clothes, her movements careful.

Was she treating Sue's things with respect, or was she just disgusted because they smelled like sweaty human? She didn't have much time to wonder. Kara was already turning to leave.

Sue sighed and walked into the little shower. She'd asked for privacy and now she had it.

The wall bore controls, written in the same language of glyphs as the monitor outside. She waved her hands at one of them and a spray of chilling cold water obligingly poured from the ceiling. She waved her fingers in front of the other, and the water warmed to a soothing heat.

She let the water flow over her a long moment, luxuriating in the feel of it on her skin, washing away the layer of grime and sweat that made her feel so dirty compared to her illuminated hosts. The water felt especially good on her leg, soothing away the tightness and the ache.

She found a small, oblong bottle of liquid she assumed counted as soap. She opened it, wary, and sniffed at it. She still wasn't sure the aliens had skin like humans did. Who knew what they used to clean themselves, or whether they'd been able to find some human-cleaning soap somewhere out here? Wherever out here was.

They're not "the aliens." They're the Outcasts.

Why had she thought that? This wasn't Earth, or any of the colonies, and they certainly weren't human. And Kara had called her people that, but she still didn't know if that was their name for themselves or not.

She dabbed a little of the soap, or whatever it was, on her forearm and let it rinse away. It lathered and bubbled like soap, and didn't sting. She waited another moment, shrugged, and slathered it over her body.

She wished she could have asked Kara. She wished Kara were here, behind her, those golden eyes boring into her back.

Would she like what she saw? Sue wasn't pretty, or she'd never thought she was. Not skinny enough, her skin too pocked with dark little spots. But had Kara even seen a human before? She'd seemed intrigued.

Did Kara take showers? Sue guessed she would have to. Otherwise she wouldn't have found a shower in here, and would have had to ask for some kind of basin and climb into it.

A little shiver ran up her back at the thought of Kara's gray skin with water beading on it. What would it do to those little cracks of light on Kara's body? Were they some kind of flame that water might put out?

Not put out. They were part of Kara, and she wouldn't just go cold.

What exactly are you made of?

She ran her fingers through her hair. They snagged on a tangle and she looked around, realizing she'd forgotten about shampoo. But there wasn't anything else around. Which only made sense. The aliens—the Outcasts—didn't have hair. Sue lathered some of the soap into her hair and squinched her eyes shut tight, just in case alien soap would sting her eyes.

It didn't. It lathered and rinsed perfectly fine, and Sue wondered again how much Kara knew about humans, and why she would take so much care with this one.

Chapter Four

Sue lounged on the cot, waiting for Kara. For better or for worse, she had something to prove now. Kara's weird theories about humans made no sense.

And, okay, maybe she also wanted to show off. Ever since Kara had stared at her before, she'd wondered: Was Kara doing all of this because she had a thing for humans?

Well, if she did, she'd find Sue trying her best to look sexy.

With emphasis on the trying. The one thing Sue hadn't found was a hairbrush. Which made perfect sense, as no one who'd passed by had hair. But it meant Sue had to do the best she could with her fingers. She hadn't quite ended up with flowing tresses.

Then again, she thought, dragging her fingers through a tangled lock of hair, would it matter? Did the Outcasts expect her hair to look nice? The only one she was sure had seen it was Kara.

But then there were the scars running down her leg, where they'd opened her skin and rearranged things and sewn her back together. Rich people could afford to have their scars smoothed, but not spacebus drivers. And compared to Kara, she looked so ordinary. Broken. Imperfect.

Kara has scars too.

Sue bit her lip. But it was true, wasn't it? And she was sensitive about them, too, just like Sue was about hers. Even those bright yellow streaks—were those scars too?

The soft hiss of the door opening interrupted her thoughts. She looked up to see Kara, cradling Sue's clean clothes in her hands. She tilted her head at the doorframe and it slid open.

"Your…clothes," she said and dropped them on the floor in front of Sue.

Well, that was fine. They'd have no time to get too wrinkled, since Sue was about to put them on. And besides, there was no place to hang them up anyway.

But was that it? After that whole conversation about shame, Kara wasn't even going to look at her?

The horned head snapped up, and the golden eyes fixed on Sue. They brightened, and Sue shivered as Kara's gaze moved down her body. It lingered on her breasts, her nipples, her hips.

Sue could guess why. Or could have if her head wasn't buzzing and her skin wasn't buzzing with energy. Kara's nipples were the same color as the rest of her, while Sue's were a dusky pink against light brown skin.

And Kara didn't have hair anywhere.

But was this just curiosity, or was it something more? Sue lifted a leg and lowered it again, watching Kara watch the movement. Kara didn't blink, and the corner of her lip turned up in the beginning of a smile.

Sue didn't realize until a moment later that it was her scarred leg she'd moved. Apparently Kara didn't care.

Come here, dammit. Come here and look at me for real.

"Did you wish to dress?" Kara pointed down at the clothes.

"Oh. Right." Well. Sue must have misread that. Or Kara wasn't sure what she wanted. Sue slipped off the bed, not bothering to try to look sultry any more, and snatched up her bra and underwear.

She faced Kara as she put them on. Maybe she wasn't going to respond to direct provocation, but Sue had seen that look.

"See?" Sue said. "I'm not ashamed."

That little half smile again. "No. You're not."

Sue grinned back and stepped into her pants. She slid the shirt over her head; for a moment, it blocked out the sight of Kara's brightening eyes.

She tugged at the fabric to smooth it down over her stomach. Her fingers caught on the scratch Kara had torn in it. She picked at it and looked over at Kara. Kara watched her without blinking, also looking at the mark.

Sue's skin underneath had a mark too, where the tip of Kara's claw had snagged her. The little scrape had already scabbed over, but it still stung when the fabric rubbed against it.

Sue frowned at it. Kara was still dangerous. These people were still dangerous, if they were anything like her. And Kara had been the nicest. The most welcoming. The most curious.

Groups were even worse. Sue had seen it. People who'd been nice enough to her and decent to others, going nuts when the right asshole with a bullhorn riled them up.

She closed her eyes, and a memory blazed against the backs of her eyelids. A young boy, shoved to the asphalt by a hard kick.

As far as Sue could tell he hadn't done anything. Just had the wrong color patches from the wrong colonies sewn to his jacket and pants. The wrong color skin. The wrong hairstyle. The wrong accent, when he pleaded with them to let him go.

Sue had wanted to help. She'd hoped to be a soldier, and that's what soldiers did. Or what soldiers should do, anyway. Protect the innocent. Defend the vulnerable. But the crowd had already gone crazy, and when hands had reached for her next, she'd panicked and ran.

As best she could. She still remembered the drag of her leg behind her, the thudding of her heart. *They'll catch me they'll catch me they'll catch me they already caught him they'll catch me anyway so why didn't I do something?*

Sue blinked the memory away, the boy's blood on the pavement a red spray behind her eyelids that she couldn't quite banish.

Kara wasn't like that mob. Kara had stopped.

"So. Unashamed one."

Sue's head snapped up. There was laughter in Kara's voice. Laughter, and the beginnings of respect. *Thank goodness.*

But why? What was Kara seeing in her, right now, with barely-combed hair and torn clothes, trying to shiver away a bad memory that wouldn't leave?

Unashamed one. What else was she supposed to be? Intrepid explorer, brave visitor, strange life form from far away. But could Sue play at being those things when wrong moves got you a claw in the belly?

Do you like humans—do you like me—or did you just not want to see someone get hurt?

"We were exploring," Kara said. "Before. When…" She reached out and touched Sue's shirt, tracing a fingertip over the tear in the fabric. Then she slipped her finger into it and pressed her fingertip against Sue's skin.

It was warm, warm like before. Sue shivered under the touch.

Kara nodded and pulled her hand away. Sue blinked at the loss and swallowed hard. Was that how an Outcast apologized?

Sue cleared her throat and straightened up again. "Yeah. We were exploring."

"We could go back out now. If you wish. If you do not—"

"Well, I can't go home. Not yet. Unless there's something you aren't telling me."

"The rifts come and go with the storms. There will be another, sometime. Perhaps a week, at the earliest. You can return home when one appears." The light in her eyes flickered, and the streaks of gold at her neck and shoulders dimmed. "If you wish to."

You don't want me to leave, do you?

If nothing else, it would be worth finding out why. Sue knew what wrong moves might get her. But what about the right ones? She took a step closer to Kara and willed herself to ignore how Kara towered over her.

Unashamed one. Why the hell not?

She reached out and laid a hand on Kara's shoulder, like she had once before. As before, Kara twitched under her hand. But this time, Kara stilled, and her lips parted in the first hint of a glowing smile.

"We were exploring," Sue said again. "Let's do some more of it."

CHAPTER FIVE

"Follow."

Sue scowled at Kara's back. Kara had said yes to exploring. Had seemed to welcome it. And now she was ordering Sue around. Like Sue was a pet dog or something. Some stray creature she'd picked up somewhere.

Sue shivered. Kara had been kind. But what if Sue was exactly that to her? A cute, lost straggler to take care of for a while, and nothing else.

She wouldn't have thought it, cold as Kara was sometimes. But then Kara had taken a swipe at her.

But Kara had admitted she'd done wrong. She hadn't apologized, not quite. But Sue still didn't know what an apology looked like on this world. Maybe that was as much of an apology as she was going to get.

And Sue still didn't know what she'd done wrong. What she'd said that upset Kara so much. These people had been banished here, and whoever had done it had seen nothing wrong with mangling their backs to punish them. What kind of memory had that stirred up?

The lights and sounds grew louder as the tunnels widened. Sue noticed fewer and fewer windows looking down on the storms and the angry planet below.

This was a place of exile. Maybe they wanted to forget.

Bright neon signs announced—what? Sue couldn't read the glyphs, and she hadn't tried. But these were clearly shops, hawking everything from furniture to new videoscreens to bowls and bottles full of liquid that Sue guessed passed for food and water.

And maybe for booze. There were restaurants, too, or something like them, and one had tables and seats set up in front of it, with people sitting at them drinking the liquids.

She watched a noisy group pass a bowl of something orange between them, laughing with brightly lit mouths. Shadows danced around them in a riot of patterns. One of them held up a clawed hand and hissed, striking out at air, and the others laughed. One of his companions clapped him on the shoulder, grinning, careful not to hit the scar on his back.

Sue looked at Kara, at the clawed hand at her side. If this was how they played, Kara lashing out at her might not be all that surprising.

Who are these people, and why were they sent away?

You know already, a part of her whispered. And on the heels of that thought, a chilling feeling.

"Are we going to get anything to eat? Er, drink?" She wasn't sure she wanted to sit near the rowdy aliens, but her stomach rumbled at the sight of food. Even weird alien food she wouldn't have a chance to chew. Her soupy dinner last night, and her breakfast this morning, had both tasted good, cool and bracing. And just drinking them had made her feel refreshed.

She had a feeling those were the alien equivalent of health food. What did the good stuff taste like? And if the health food made you feel comfortable right away, what would decadent treats do? Sue's mouth watered.

And she hadn't seen Kara drink anything, and now that she knew the aliens ate the same stuff Kara had given her, she felt worried.

Worried and protective. Kara had protected her. Fretting in return was the least she could do. Even if she had no idea how to take care of a gorgeous naked giant alien who knew far more about what was going on than she did.

Kara frowned. "You have no need for other food right now. The drink I gave you was the best thing we have to restore your strength, Sue."

I don't need anything else? I'm a visitor, not a child.

But there were other things to see, and Sue might as well have been a child, wide as her eyes got.

Some people looked back at her, their eyes bright pinpricks of flame. Most were wide with what Sue assumed was curiosity, but some burned under slanted, angry brows. The penumbral auras around them whirled and danced with their agitation.

One, a slim female with skin almost as dark as Kara's, broad curling horns, and skin-cracks the orange of a warm fire, growled as Sue passed. Her voice had the same hollow echo as Kara's, but the snarl overlaid it, a bestial noise, almost like she had two voices.

Sue huddled closer to Kara, and her head lowered. *No. I'm stuck here. I can't show them weakness.*

She raised her head, high and proud, the kind of posture she'd always imagined a starfighter pilot would stand in. She straightened up, evening her stride, forcing her bad leg to limp as little as possible by sheer force of will alone. These people might have been Outcasts, but she was the outsider, and determined not to show it made her weak.

Besides, this was supposed to be an adventure, and if she let it terrify her, she'd miss everything there was to see.

A group of musicians gathered around another of the corridors. They hummed, a haunting lilt, and Sue closed her eyes and stopped walking. Their voices echoed, like Kara's, but it fit the eerie music. Could all the aliens sing like that?

Then someone began to play an instrument.

Sue had always liked imagining to music, always found it easy. The reverberations of the music and the singer's melancholy tone wove through her mind. And the images came like she didn't even have to try to picture it at all. Tall mountains, sunlight gilding them.

The bright orange-red of a sunrise or a sunset. She could feel its warmth. The coarseness of sand under her feet. She could feel that too, a roughness between her toes.

She'd never actually seen mountains, only pictures of them. Or been in open space like that. In the colonies, everyone lived and moved in crowds.

Was this really her imagination, or was she seeing what the singers wanted her to?

People walked down from the foot of the mountains. They were tall like the aliens, but instead of stony gray skin, theirs shone in warm pinks and browns, gilded by the orange light of the sun. Almost but not quite metallic, without bright cracks in their skin either. The horns were gone too, only a pair of faint ridges in their foreheads testifying to where they'd been.

They had no hair. Or at least, Sue couldn't tell if they did. Light radiated out from behind their heads in glowing coronas. She couldn't tell what color it was either. It shone so bright all that registered was light, all color seared away by its brightness. She guessed its tone was warm, but it was too much for her eyes.

For human eyes, she guessed.

I'm only human.

Maybe the beings in this—vision?—weren't aliens at all. Maybe Sue really was just imagining things, mixing up the new world she'd found with the old world she'd left behind.

And was starting to miss, if she really thought about it. The singer wailed another note and Sue felt it, a melancholy chill. These people weren't real, weren't hers, and she was far from home.

The people opened their eyes, and their eyes were almost human: deep, rich browns, verdant greens, piercing blues, pale grays. But they glowed with the same inner light as the aliens' bodies. The insides of their mouths glowed too. Not the furnace-reds and flame-golds of the aliens, but a warm, inviting white.

The white wrapped around them too, curled up around their backs in a bright halo. It shimmered, feather-gossamer. The singers wailed in loss: a rumbling bass that made Sue fear the ground in her vision might split, a piercing soprano that stung her ears.

Then the people in Sue's vision unfurled spans of light behind them.

They moved, smooth as cloth. And they glowed, so bright a white that Sue couldn't quite focus on them. They rose behind their owners, feathery coronas of light. They moved, up and down, and the people hovered just above the ground, dust and sand curling below them.

"Wings," Sue said out loud, shattering the illusion. The vision dissolved, leaving her facing a group of people with stone skin, holding musical instruments in their hands, light peeking through cracks in their flesh.

She looked over at Kara's back, at the two misshapen stumps at her shoulders and the bright, noxious gleam of the scars. Shadows swirled around her, a faint remembrance of something that had once been there.

"Wings," Sue said again. "You used to have wings."

CHAPTER SIX

Sue shrank from Kara in fear. Twisted stumps where wings had been. Claws. Horns. Eerie light glowing through the cracks in stony skin.

We are outcasts, Kara had said.

Yes, I'm sure you were.

Sue stumbled backward, panic building, her throat beginning to tighten and her leg throbbing like it had finally remembered to hurt. Kara was looking at her, golden eyes wide, but she couldn't think of that, couldn't focus, couldn't go to her, not when—

"Interesting. Is this some kind of pet?"

Sue's head snapped up. She didn't like the sound of that, especially not in Weird Alien Intonation. But Kara sounded like that too. And however ominous the reverberations might sound, the tone was mocking, not threatening. Dismissive.

Another Outcast was looking at her, his skin ash pale, his streaks of light a fiery red. He looked slimmer than Kara and some of the others around them. Young, maybe? His lips were curled in a sneer and he blinked down at Sue as if surprised by what he saw.

"I'm not a pet," Sue blurted. Part of her still wanted to hide behind Kara, but that would only make this worse. And if Kara really was what she suspected, Kara might not be all that safe either.

"This human is mine for the moment, Dehek," Kara spat back.

"Did you get it from down below?" He leaned down to sniff at her. "Down on the dunes? In one of the flame pits? She doesn't smell like either of them."

Down below? Sue tensed. Kara had said that only the oldest Outcast would know about humans.

"That is none of your concern." Kara's tone, even colder and more sepulchral than usual, pulled Sue from her thoughts.

Dehek's shadows drew in tighter around him. Then he smirked. "But, Kara, you shouldn't be adopting strays." His nostrils flared. A red light flickered in them. "Every human on the surface is there for a reason. But she's not from the surface, is she? She smells too fresh for that."

Every human on the surface.

There are humans down there. And everybody knows about them.

The musicians turned toward Sue. Their eyes glowed with obvious interest, and the streaks on their skin pulsed. Sue winced.

Kara snarled, a rumbling sound that didn't fit the stately, glowing body Sue saw in front of her. She shuddered, imagining fur and fangs and wild things with wide snouts stained in blood.

Was that another vision or something else these...beings could do?

"I'm not from down there!" Sue cried.

She stood straighter, trying to look confident. If she was going to get in the middle of this, she might as well go all the way.

"I'm not from your planet," she finished. "Or from your Rings, or whatever you call them. I'm from one of Earth's colonies, and—" She snapped her mouth shut. *I'm from one of Earth's colonies* was too much information already.

"Of course you are." Dehek sneered. "You'd never make it up here if you weren't lost."

Kara's eyes glowed, and her lips curled back. "Leave the human alone."

"Why, Kara, it sounds almost like you don't want her to know where she is."

Kara snarled again. She dropped into a crouch and held her clawed hands out, ready to attack or to defend.

Sue shivered thinking of the rioting back home. They'd almost knocked her down once, with her bad leg slowing her down. And that young boy, the one she couldn't help. In her memory, his eyes went wide, he sobbed and pleaded.

And she had to run away or she'd be next.

She closed her eyes and could see the hands reaching for her. "Really, guys. I'm not worth all this."

Kara ignored her. "Who exactly do you think you are? I was there in the beginning. Were you?"

"There in the beginning," Dehek answered. He crouched down too, a lazy movement, laced with scorn. "Do you think that makes you special?"

"I think it makes me more than you, little warrior," Kara said and lunged.

Her claws flashed out and bit deep into Dehek's skin. Sue saw it flake away from the wound. Maybe they really are made of stone, Sue thought, and shuddered.

She couldn't peel her eyes away. She'd felt like this once before, watching someone shove a young boy to the ground. The punches, the kicks, the blood—

But now there was no blood. Only a small ooze of clear, thick ichor and the red light that his skin covered, now exposed. Like one of the streaks, only bigger and angrier and obviously painful.

He lashed back at Kara, aiming at her belly, but she twisted away and the claws just grazed her. Sue saw faint lines of gold appear against her dark skin and winced.

Dehek crouched, his lips twisted in pain or rage or both, his claws still held out to strike. Kara followed suit, laughing, gesturing for him to attack again, as if all this were nothing more than some minor nuisance.

"Stop!" Sue cried again. "Whatever you're arguing about, I'm just a guest."

"The creature is right," someone rumbled.

Sue turned around and found herself facing a tall, broad alien—Outcast—with dark skin like Kara's and thick, twisting horns. His eyes and the streaks in his skin burned orange.

But Dehek either wasn't listening or didn't care. He rushed at Kara from the side, apparently intent on revenge. Kara twisted away and kicked him, hard enough that he fell to the ground with a rumbling cry.

She inclined her head to the other Outcast. "I apologize for his bad manners."

Dehek turned his head and hissed, his lips drawing back. His teeth were dark and pointed against the bright red of his mouth. He scrambled to his feet, an animal's clamber, and dashed off again.

Sue felt warmth spread through her despite her fear. Kara had driven off someone who meant to hurt her.

The big Outcast wasn't as impressed. His hairless eyebrow ridges creased, and he cast a significant look down the hall where Dehek had fled. "You apologize for his bad manners? You brought a human here. A quickened one."

"Sue is telling the truth. She is stranded. What else could I have done?"

"You could have left her. Humans do not make good pets. They don't belong here. Not living ones, anyway."

Sue shivered. Not living ones? Was this guy saying he wanted her dead? He wasn't threatening her, not like Dehek had, but whatever that meant, it wasn't good. And "do not make good pets"? What was that about?

The male Outcast was still staring down the hall. "And that fool was right about one thing."

"What is that?" Kara asked, her voice cold.

"An elder warrior like you should know better than to keep pets."

Kara growled, a low and thunderous hum. She grabbed at Sue's hand. "Come. We're leaving. Now."

Chapter Seven

"So now I'm a pet?"

Kara blinked but didn't answer. That was bad.

"Tell me," Sue said. "What was that guy talking about? Dehek, or whatever his name was?"

"Dehek is a fool. Made too late to understand what is happening around him."

"Made too late?"

"He is young. He knows nothing. Nothing of the worlds beyond this and nothing of his own purpose."

Sue rolled her eyes. "I'm not even going to pretend to know what that means. And it wasn't just Dehek."

"He began this."

"Yeah. He did. But it wasn't just him. The big guy said 'humans don't make good pets.' Like humans are just hard to take care of or something."

The corner of Kara's lip quirked up in a smile. "Hard to take care of? Do you find fault with the way I've cared for you?"

"What? No! No."

"Then what do you mean?"

Sue put her hands on her hips. "I mean I'm a human, Kara. Not a dog. Not a cat. Not some kind of robot companion."

"I'm aware that you are human." Kara stepped closer. "But why be so offended? What exactly were you expecting, Sue Jones?"

Sue blinked. What was she expecting? She'd gotten caught in a wormhole, not sought out a distant world that welcomed tourists. And where she'd found herself, if she was right about Kara and the others, wasn't a place she'd choose to be.

"This world is ours," Kara was saying. She flexed her clawed fingers, and Sue stared in fascination. Whatever Kara was, she was still beautiful.

And Sue's body still responded. She felt her cheeks flush and cursed under her breath.

"We don't welcome humans on this planet," Kara finished.

"And that means it's all right to treat me like this?"

"I treat you better than the others. They wouldn't want anything to do with humans. Not unless—"

"Not unless they were down on the surface?" Sue snapped. "Battered by storms? Burning in a flame pit?"

She clapped a hand around her mouth and stepped back. The pristine room felt wrong. A polished, gilded cage, trapping her alone with—

She shuddered. She could feel the word in the back of her throat, like something she needed to cough up. But if she said it, she might make it real.

Kara didn't notice or didn't care. She tilted her head, all innocence. "What are you talking about?"

"That's what Dehek said, isn't it? 'She's not from the surface, is she?'"

"Dehek is a fool."

"But you do have humans on the surface. You're not denying it." Sue shuddered. "Down there."

Kara nodded, a crisp, cold movement. "We do. And the more of the Outcasts who see you, the more of them will wonder whether you belong there. And whether I think so. Or why I don't."

Sue's eyes widened in shock and horror. She tried to imagine it. Remembered the riots back home. The violence, the screaming, the beating, the flames. "No one could survive down there!"

Was that what Dehek meant? He'd said something about how she smelled. But Sue wasn't sure what. Smelled good? Smelled healthy? Smelled like someone who wasn't stranded on a dead planet exposed to the elements?

"You are right. No one could survive down there. Why do you think we built these Rings?"

Anger flared through Sue. "So you people, you Outcasts, get banished down here for God knows what—"

"Don't." Kara's lips drew back in a snarl. Bright light flared between her teeth.

But Sue wasn't finished. "Get tossed down here, and someone tears your fucking wings off—"

Kara raised her hands, claws poised to strike. "Don't."

Kara's eyes flickered. Sue slid to the side, trying to make sure Kara couldn't corner her if she lashed out again. But she didn't stop talking. "Tossed down here, and the first thing you do is throw humans down to—"

"Only the dead ones," Kara cut in.

"Dead ones?"

"You think there are living humans here?"

"I don't think anything."

"If there were, I would have taken you to them. And left you with them, if the others had anything to say about it."

Dead ones. Sue looked around the room again. It didn't look like a room for the dead. It was better maintained than any room Sue had ever been in. But it was for the Outcasts. Not the humans they kept, whether as pets or as—

Prey.

From what Dehek had said this morning, and what the musicians' song had shown her, it made a twisted kind of sense. She backed away from Kara, her eyes wide.

"Dead ones. You were banished from where you lived before, had your wings torn off, and you keep dead humans down on the surface of some awful torture planet. With storms, and maybe fire."

"We—"

Sue looked up and stared straight at Kara. At her horns, her glowing eyes, the harsh angles of her sculpted body. At the lines of gold running over her stony skin. Like scars. Like cracks. Like breaks.

At the mist of shadows wrapping around Kara's back, where a gleaming set of white wings used to be.

"I know what you are!" Sue said at last.

Kara's head snapped up. She growled, a dark rumble. But she didn't say anything.

So Sue said it for her. "You're demons."

"We are Outcasts."

"You're demons. And what's down there is hell."

Kara growled again. "There are some human souls there, yes."

Sue stepped closer to Kara, glaring. If she'd let herself think at all, she never would have done it. Who would threaten a fallen angel?

But Sue found herself doing it, all the same. "And when exactly were you going to get around to telling me about this? After the tour?"

Kara raised her head. "You are alive. You didn't need to know."

"I didn't need to know?"

"You were stranded here."

Stranded here. And Kara had picked her up. Would anyone else have done that? Dead humans belonged down there, and a living one would die quick, from what Kara and Dehek described.

Why?

"I was stranded here, and you saved me. Why?"

"You were lost. Even the Enemy wouldn't punish you for that."

The Enemy. Who was that? The Outcasts' leader, or the God that Sue barely remembered, so much more important to her mother and her father than to her?

Sue stepped closer to Kara again, still glaring up at her. "And you were going to tell me this when exactly?"

"Once you had seen our world. Once you understood it. Once you did some exploring, as you wished to."

"Exploring. I take a wrong turn somewhere past the edge of the Rim and wind up in hell, and you think I want to go exploring?"

Kara turned toward one of the windows and looked out. "Didn't you?"

"Yes, before I knew it was hell!"

Kara snorted, a beast's sound, and shook her head. "It isn't hell. Or at least, it's not what you think hell is."

"What is that supposed to mean?"

Kara cut her off with a wave of her hand. "Look around you. At where you are now. At the Rings. Does this look like the hell your people know?"

Sue looked around. Sheltering walls, half clear glass, half metal, polished and gleaming. Did demons build cities? She'd heard names sometimes, in really old books, for the places in hell where the monsters gathered.

But did they look like this? Like something from the colonies, only better made and cleaner? Maintained, not cracking like the concrete or rusting like the metal back home?

"No," Sue said finally. "No. This doesn't look like hell."

Kara walked over to Sue's cot and sat down. The shadowy mist she carried curled around her, and she lowered her head again. Sue reached out, her hands itching to touch, to soothe.

What am I doing?

Kara looked up. "You humans know many things about us. You've heard many things about our origin and our history. Some of it is true. I won't deny that. But there is also much that you have forgotten. Or lost."

Sue hesitated, her hand hovering over Kara's skin. What Kara said made sense. If someone had ripped her wings off and thrown her to some awful planet, maybe even worse than the worlds the colonies were built on, she'd be furious too.

And yet.

Demons were supposed to be tempting. Demons were supposed to sound convincing. Demons were supposed to worm their way into your mind and make you think everything they said sounded right.

But before Sue could put her hand down, Kara grabbed it. Stony fingers wrapped around Sue's, and the tips of sharp claws pressed against the back of her hand.

"Listen to me," Kara said.

But she didn't say anything more. Instead, she pulled Sue closer.

What are you doing?

But Kara's face lingered inches from hers, and she knew exactly what Kara was doing. Around them both, the shadows danced, a whispering promise of wings.

Sue closed the distance between them. She pressed her lips to Kara's before she could think better of it.

They were thick and warm. Then Kara's lips parted, and the strange warmth made Sue moan into her mouth.

Kara's hand wrapped around the back of her head and drew her closer. She shuddered at the strength in it. Kara was a demon. What strength of will did it take not to hurt a human partner?

She's a demon. A demon is kissing me.

I'm kissing a demon.

It should have felt wrong. It should have been frightening. And somewhere deep down in Sue's brain or her heart or her gut it did, a queasy little shiver of warning. But Kara's open mouth was warm with whatever light burned inside her throat.

That thought made Sue shiver again. Who else would ever come this close to touching an angel's spirit, even a fallen one? Sue let herself twitch, rode the wave of adrenaline making her skin tingle.

Kara's hands wound in her hair and she opened her mouth wider.

CHAPTER EIGHT

"These clothes are in the way." Kara's voice echoed, low and hollow as always. But Sue heard a growl under it, an animal sound like the one she'd heard during the fight.

It almost made Sue laugh. Demons were supposed to be temptresses, whispering promises into unsuspecting human ears. And yet Kara knew so little about humans that all she could say was "why aren't you naked already?"

Sue smirked. *I might know more than a demon.* It was a heady feeling, a good one. A powerful one, in a world where Sue had no power.

She slipped off her clothes, not even trying to be sultry about it. She'd shown Kara that she wasn't ashamed already, whatever that meant. And demons didn't even wear clothes anyway, from what she'd seen and what Kara had told her before.

And this wasn't the best place to be seductive. Sue hadn't seen much of the Rings beyond this little corridor, but this was the demons' hospital.

If not where they bring sick pets.

Sue willed the thought away. Kara wanted this, wanted her. And she knew what clothes were now, and what it meant to take them off. Sue glanced over to her shirt and pants, tossed in a wrinkled heap at the foot of her cot. Sexy enough, she guessed.

Kara leaned down over her. She reached up to touch Kara's chest, anticipating its warmth. Then she felt it for real, a smooth heat that lit her fingertips.

It didn't quite feel like touching another human. It didn't quite feel real. The stony skin was smooth but not polished, leaving a hint of texture. It reminded Sue of running her hands over a rock, kept in the pocket of her jacket as a tool to calm herself.

I'm touching a demon. And it's soothing.

Kara's eyes flickered. Her lips parted, the crack of golden light between them brightening. "Your fingertips are soft."

Sue grinned. "So you do like humans. Or is it just me?" She slid her finger over Kara's skin, toward one of the bright cracks. Kara's skin was warm. Would those be hot? Would they sear her fingertips? A little thrill curled through her. She wanted to find out.

She moved her finger closer to the golden streak. Closer, closer, as close as she dared. Her fingertips warmed, like before. She closed her eyes and imagined curls of smoke and crackling flame, vivid as the images from the band's song. Was this another one of the Outcasts' powers?

It warmed her nerves, bright enough to burn, but didn't hurt.

The life force of an angel. Or someone who used to be one, anyway. Sue sucked in a breath. If one tiny crack felt like this, how would it have felt before Kara fell? Sue's lips twisted into a wry smile. The one question she could never ask: *What was it like when you were an angel?*

But she could find out, if she was brave enough to try. She bit her lip, closed her eyes, and slipped her palm directly over the glowing crack.

Her mind filled again with images of flame. The nerves in her hand tingled, the energy under her palm the crackling center of it all. It burned, too hot, but didn't harm her. There was only a cleansing ignition, searing away all other sensation and leaving only this.

Kara looked down at Sue's hand. "You're brave for a human. You should be frightened of our fire."

"So it is fire, then."

"More than fire. But I do not know how we were made. I thought I knew why, in the beginning. But now I know that I do not."

Sue shook her head and clamped her lips shut on a question. Whatever she asked now might awaken the rage she'd seen before.

Kara chuckled, amused or wry or both, and reached out to touch Sue's chest. She pressed her fingers to Sue's skin like she thought it was paper she could rip just by touching it.

Her fingers were warm. Warmer than a human's? Sue thought so. But that might just be her imagination. Or the hunger building in her flesh.

Then there were Kara's claws and the strength behind them. Sue shivered. How easily could they tear her skin? She sucked in a heavy breath, trying not to tremble, wondering whether she wanted the hands tracing over her skin to be gentle or rough.

"You're soft," Kara said. She smirked. That made Sue shiver for real, unable to repress it, however risky twitching under a demon's hands might be.

Kara noticed. "Fragile," she whispered, and laughed. Her lips drew back in a predatory grin.

"Maybe so." Sue pushed out her chest, wanting more of Kara's touch. She let herself say exactly what she was thinking. "I'm stranded here. A ring made of metal is the only thing between me and hell. And I'm in bed with a demon."

She grinned. "Go ahead."

Kara laughed again. Sue closed her eyes and gave herself up to the eerie, hollow sound. It moved through her, and she canted her hips. Might as well. After all, she had nothing to lose.

Kara curled her claws inward, just pricking Sue's skin. *I'm trusting a demon.* Sue fought down a chuckle.

Little beads of blood welled up from where Kara had pricked her. She thought of vampires, of succubi. Of the price for their sex or their love, the sweet hypnosis of their sting. In that light it felt good, a sharp prick to seal a pact. To bring them close. Maybe even to make them one.

Kara's hands stilled, and Sue saw a question in her eyes. Careful, she arched her back. *Yes. Yes.*

She slid her hand past Kara's shoulder and up to her back, careful to avoid the scars at her shoulder blades. A heaviness lingered around Kara's shoulders, a warm press of air. The shadows, Sue thought. The shadows that used to be wings.

Kara's eyes widened, and her clawed fingers stilled against Sue's skin. They bit deeper, a sharp pinch.

"Wait!" Sue cried. "I'm not going to touch you there. I promise."

The hairless brow ridges angled downward, and Sue knew the light in Kara's eyes wasn't all lust.

She moved her hand, as quickly as she dared, into the middle of Kara's back and splayed her fingers out in a sign of submission and surrender.

Kara laughed. Her claws kneaded at Sue's flesh one last time, not gently enough, but then subsided again. She lowered her head, and Sue took a ragged breath. The sound filled the space between them.

"Someday," Kara whispered. "Someday, perhaps, I will tell you."

Someday. If someday comes, I'll have been here a long time.

Kara opened her hand, slid her fingers over Sue's skin like any human lover. They slipped over her breasts and ghosted over her nipples. Sue felt them harden under Kara's touch and let out a long moan.

"Interesting." Kara chuckled again. "What else can I make you do, little human?"

Sue felt obligated to glare. She tried, but Kara was already moving again, her hands tracing the contours of Sue's stomach, pausing at the white taut skin of an old scar, and slipping farther down, toward her hips…

Sue stared up at Kara through half-lidded eyes. In her unfocused, hazy gaze, the horned, fire-eyed figure in front of her looked just like any succubus. Any temptress she'd ever heard about or read about or seen in a holomovie. Or imagined, in the middle of some too-dark night when only strange fantasies would do. Shadow-wings framed Kara's body, and her light shone gold against it.

She opened her thighs wide, wondering if lowly human skin, with its wrinkles and its softness and its smells and its dirt, could ever be enough.

But if that mattered to Kara, she gave no sign. Curious fingers slipped past Sue's hips and paused at the slick flesh they found there. Kara's eyes widened, a bright stab of gold, and then her fingers moved over Sue's labia. Sue twitched and arched her hips, half in response and half to say *this, yes, good.*

But Kara wasn't Sue's dream succubus. Demon or no, Kara was a person, a real one, with her own body. And its own needs, if fallen angels were anything like humans. Sue reached out her other arm and wrapped it around Kara's back, a jolt of sensation running through her arm and wrist as they cut through the mist of shadows around her.

Kara shook her head. Sue froze. She wanted to touch Kara, wanted to make Kara feel something. But she was a stranger here, a human in a world for beings who were so much more than that.

All right. I'll wait.

Kara pulled her fingers away. Sue whimpered at the loss. But Kara only held them up, Sue's wetness glistening on them, and turned them back and forth, studying them.

"You don't have…?" Sue tried.

"We do. But not like this. Not quite." Kara raised her fingers to her nose and sniffed at them. Sue thought of the pungent scent, and a thrill of nervousness ran through her. But Kara just favored her with a lopsided grin.

"Let me see what you have," Sue said, emboldened.

Kara laughed and lowered her hand to Sue's flesh again. "Perhaps. Not yet."

But before Sue could ask about that, Kara ran her fingers over Sue's labia again and then slipped them between them. Sue gasped and forgot to argue. Kara snickered, paused a moment at Sue's entrance, and pushed her fingers in.

Sue gasped out a welcome and bucked against Kara's fingers. Maybe that was risky, maybe that was dangerous. She'd seen those claws. But she'd also chosen this, agreed to this, and now she wanted everything.

Kara's fingers inside her felt both foreign and familiar. Like anything else, anyone else, filling her up and beginning to move. But the texture felt different, unyielding as stone, hard enough to claim her, to take more than any human lover ever had.

And Kara's fingers were warm, filled with her inner fire. Sue looked up at Kara leaning down over her. It blazed from the cracks in her shoulders, in her chest, and smoldered in her hungry eyes.

Yes, Sue thought, yes, and screamed it aloud, not caring how she sounded. This was no world she knew, and only someone more than human would hear it anyway. Her hand curled against Kara's back, her fingernails digging into the space where a human's spine would be.

Kara laughed again. Her thumb moved to Sue's clit and thrilled there even as her fingers slipped deeper.

Sue tried to keep her eyes open. She wanted to look back at Kara, stare into those burning, alien eyes. But Kara pulled her thumb away again, a loss that made Sue throw back her head and keen again.

Then Kara drove her fingers into Sue, fast and rough, heedless of Sue's delicate flesh. Sue froze, locked around Kara's fingers, and then spasmed hard, again and again and again.

CHAPTER NINE

Sue floated in a haze. Her sex spasmed with the rhythm of aftershock. She stared up at the ceiling, the bluish-tinted lights. Where was she? No place on the colony looked this clean, and she couldn't remember that color.

She blinked unfocused eyes, watched blurry shadows chase themselves across her vision. That was familiar. A dark silhouette hovered over her, streaks of gold glittering in its midst. Was this a dream?

Kara. She rubbed her eyes. "Seems you like humans after all."

Kara laughed. "Fair enough."

"Then come here."

Kara only chuckled. But she sat on the edge of Sue's little cot, all the same.

"We'll have to find a bigger bed," Sue teased her. Kara grinned back. "Now let me touch you." Sue reached out and wrapped her hands around Kara's back, careful to avoid her shoulders. The shadowy remnants of Kara's wings were warm, as before, the heat and the heavy air reminding Sue they'd once had real weight. She wrapped her hands around Kara's sides and slid them down, trying to be as sensual as Kara had been before.

She looked up at Kara, studying her reaction. Then she saw her reward: a flicker in Kara's eyes, a slight part of her thick lips. Sue sat up straighter, eager. Kara might have been a demon, an alien, a strange being whose origin Sue could only guess at and Sue's old religion probably didn't answer either. But Kara was a woman, and Kara wanted her, and that was all that really mattered.

A bruising grip around her wrists stopped her. Sue yelped, half in pain and half in surprise. "Kara, what…?"

"Not now."

"You keep saying that. What the hell do you mean?"

The grip on Sue's wrists lessened. Then Kara let go entirely. Stung and still aching, Sue pulled her hands away and rubbed at her sore wrists.

Kara reached out a hand to cup Sue's face. Sue flinched, feeling the claws against her skin. Her earlier elation was gone. Kara was still a demon, and that still meant something. Had she meant to be that rough, or did she just not know her own strength?

"Sue," Kara said, in the kind of soothing tone Sue might have expected of a succubus, "surely you're pleased with what just happened."

"Yes. Yes, of course. But why won't you let me touch you?"

Kara's claw traced its way down her neck. Sue shuddered, not sure whether she was feeling desire all over again or recoiling.

"You are quite good enough without needing to touch me in return," Kara said, still sliding her fingertip over Sue's neck in the same lulling dance.

"Good enough? Good enough at what? I'm not even doing anything. You won't let me!"

"I only meant—"

"Good enough? Or do you mean entertaining enough?"

Kara's fingers froze. "What do you mean?"

"I mean I told you I'm not a pet, and you didn't answer."

"Human."

Sue snorted. "See? There it is. 'Human.' Just 'human.' Like I could be anyone. Like some kind of creature."

"Sue."

"Thanks."

Kara just stared at her.

Sue tried not to let it bother her. "Now tell me, what exactly was that guy Dehek talking about?"

"I told you already, hu…Sue. Dehek is a fool who thinks only of himself. He finds his pride in sneering at the dead ones, because he knows what we have lost." Kara looked down. "And he is young. He wasn't one of us. Wasn't one of the army that failed and fell."

"He lost his wings. Like the rest of you."

"Yes."

"But you just said he was too young."

"That is also true. He was born after our revolt."

"But then he never fell." Sue shuddered, thinking of it. She didn't like Dehek at all, but for an Outcast he was just a kid. A braggart. A swaggering little bully.

And sure, that was bad. Especially since Sue was only human. What terrible things could a rude brat do, if that rude brat was a demon?

Sue winced, remembering the fight. He'd thought she was one of the dead ones. He might want her to be, after Kara had humiliated him.

But did he really deserve those scars, ripped across his back? That incorporeal darkness, a memory of wings he'd never had?

Or, Sue thought with another violent shudder, wings he'd had and lost.

"All of our kin are born fallen, Sue," Kara said. "Even the young ones. No Outcast is innocent."

"That's horrible!"

But even as she yelled it, something in the back of her mind said *Salvation is for God's people. Fallen angels can't repent. They had their chance.*

"Born paying for their mothers' and their fathers' sins." Kara reached up, past her own shoulders, toward her back.

"Don't!" Sue cried. But Kara's clawed fingertips had already curled around her scar and slipped over it, again and again, running across the length of the scar and then beginning again.

Sue didn't know what to say. How did you comfort a fallen angel who missed her wings? Whatever Sue said, it would be wrong. It would never be enough. Not quite. So she cleared her throat and said the only thing she could think of instead. "Do you regret it?"

Kara laughed, a bitter, choked echo. "No. No. I don't regret it. No more than the one who led us."

The one who led them. Sue gulped and remembered Kara's claw against her skin. She almost wanted it back. The one who led them. The leader of the rebellion. The Lord of the Demons.

The greatest enemy humanity had ever had. If you believed the old religion, anyway. Sue looked around. Metal and glass. And computers, filled with scrolling pictures and words. Just like the colonies. Just like home.

Clearly, the old religion didn't know everything.

"I don't regret it," Kara said again. "I would do it again, if we got another chance." Her other hand curled, and her voice became a monstrous growl. Sue closed her eyes and saw swiping claws, a mist of red spraying the space behind her eyelids, a curled, still form on pavement, stained with blood.

It reminded her of home and made her wonder if the hell below was worse. Their Enemy is lucky he's a god, Sue thought before she could stop herself.

"You'd do that again?" she said instead. She didn't actually know what "that" was, not really, but she wasn't sure what else to say. "Even though you lost?"

"It would be foolish. It would only bring us pain." Kara growled. Her grip tightened over her scar, and Sue reached out reflexively.

"Don't hurt yourself!" she tried. But Kara's grip on her own scar only tightened, and she hissed like she'd dug in too hard.

Could angels bleed? She hadn't seen blood when Kara cut Dehek, only his skin peeling and flaking away, exposing the light beneath. She shuddered. Kara's scar was already so raw.

Sue curled her fingers around Kara's hand, her grip as tight as she could make it. It probably meant nothing to a warrior demon, but she had to try. "Please. Stop."

Kara stared back at Sue, the light in her eyes suddenly dull. That wasn't good, but it might at least mean Kara had given up on hurting herself. Sue pulled Kara's hand away from her scar, and Kara didn't resist. She let Sue guide her hand back down to her side and lay it down against her thigh.

Sue let go and ran her fingers over the back of Kara's hand. Kara's eyes narrowed, and Sue couldn't tell if they brightened or not, but it looked like she'd relaxed, at least. "There you go," she said, just like she'd soothe an angry rider on her bus. "Whatever happened, you don't need to relive it."

Kara shook her horned head. "No. No, I don't." The corner of her mouth turned up. "Not for a human."

Sue glared at her. She could live with Kara making jokes about humans. But… "You still haven't told me what Dehek meant. And every time I ask you—"

Kara lifted her head. She slipped her hand out from under Sue's and copied the gesture, running her fingers over the back of Sue's hand and then sliding them higher, over her wrist and forearm. She curled her fingertips inward and skated the tips of her claws over Sue's skin.

"Would it be so bad, Sue Jones, to be my pet?"

Chapter Ten

"Damn it, Kara, I'm not interested in being anyone's pet!" Sue waved her arms in frustration.

Things had been going so well. She was touching Kara, Kara was touching her. She'd managed to make Kara feel better, after…whatever that was. The bad memories. Sue knew plenty about those. And what she knew had helped.

Hell, Kara might even have wanted her again, once she felt calmer. And then…that. Again.

Was that why Kara had rescued her in the first place? Just so she could keep her, like an animal or a possession?

Kara's hand locked over her arm. Not a bruising grip, but tight enough to remind Sue that Kara wasn't used to being gainsaid.

"What do you think you are here, Sue Jones?"

By now, Sue knew Kara's voice, her glow, the claws, the shadow around her that once had been wings. But that tone was different, cold as a tomb and with a barbed monster roar somewhere beneath the sound. Even the room felt chilled.

"What do I think I am?" Sue repeated, feeling small.

"You are a living human. In a place where only dead ones belong. And the dead ones are here for punishment. For absolution, if they can find it." She scowled. "Most never do."

The dead. Sue thought of the storms, the winds. Would she ever see them? Could she, even? The Rings served as a shelter. Built by fallen angels. They looked so normal. Glass, metal, computer screens. Nothing like the citadels of hell Sue imagined when she heard tales of the lake of fire or looked at pictures of ancient tapestries.

But could she even go and look if she wanted? Her shuttle was here somewhere. Was it badly wrecked? Would the Outcasts bother to repair it? And even if they did, was it made of the same sturdy stuff as the demons' city? Or would it fall apart if she ever tried to fly down there?

If she ever tried to discover what the Outcasts really did to people like her.

She looked over at Kara and shuddered. "You're saying most of them think of me like Dehek does."

"I'm saying most of them won't think of you at all."

"But you took me out. To the city, or the market, or whatever it was."

"Yes."

"Why do it?"

Kara tilted her head. "What?"

"Why save me? The others would have left me. You didn't. And they thought—what? That I was a dead soul you'd taken with you?"

"Perhaps. But Dehek could smell you, remember? Smell your living flesh. As could the others. As can I, if that really matters."

"Then they knew."

"They knew you were lost. That you were a—"

"A stray," Sue finished for her.

Kara stared straight at Sue, her eyes wide. "What do you mean?"

"A lost dog." Sue spat the words. "A creature. A lost animal, to take in and take care of."

Kara stared at Sue and tilted her head with infuriating innocence. "What of it?"

"I'm a person, Kara, not an animal."

"You are a mortal."

What was Sue supposed to say to that?

"You're a human. You breathe air. You eat other creatures, plant or animal. You cannot survive without consuming. Even if you could, in the end you would still pass away. You are young, for your kind. But even now, you bear the marks of injuries your flesh and your muscles and your bones cannot heal."

She stared down at Sue lying on the bed, looking at her side. "Did you really think I never noticed your leg?"

Dammit.

"You are a mortal, Sue Jones. We may be Outcasts, still paying for our sins against our Enemy, but to beings like you, we might as well be gods."

Kara closed her eyes. Then she hummed, a shapeless note. Wistful like the singers before, though she didn't have their instruments.

Or their voices, by angels' standards. Sue knew enough by now to tell that Kara was no singer. Still, to Sue it was beautiful, the memory of an existence Sue could only guess at.

The light bleeding through her cracks shimmered, suddenly bright. It poured forth from them, wreathing her in brightness, the shadow of her remembered wings a dark corona around the light.

The shadow and light merged, a feathery shape, black against white weaving one into the other. Sue knew before the dream-image came what she would see: a woman, her skin dark brown, shimmering and almost metallic. Her eyes were brown too, but shone with coppery light, little hints of Kara's. A halo, like a sunburst, glowed behind her head. And behind her back flared her wings, a blaze of white light so bright Sue couldn't make out their shape. She saw only white, a shape somewhere between a flicker of feathers and a sunburst.

The light curled around her like her shadows. But it moved with her. These were her wings. These were real. Were a part of her body, not just hints of limbs she'd lost millennia ago. She spread them out in a burst of light that stung Sue's eyes.

There were no cracks in her skin to reveal her inner fire, but the play of light on her skin promised it nonetheless, faint waves dancing over it like water when she moved. And Sue could see it in her eyes, in her nose, pouring from her open mouth.

Her horns were gone too, the same faint ridges she'd seen on the dancers' foreheads the only hint of where they'd been. Sue's hands twitched with a sudden desire to run over the bumps.

I can't. Sue tightened her hands into fists. The thing in front of her wasn't something a human had any right to touch.

Or even to behold. Not really. Not without an occasion, an event, world-shattering news that would change the lives of puny humans forever. She'd heard their song before, and that was more of a blessing than she would ever deserve.

"I'm sorry," she said, closing her eyes and lowering her head.

Kara's humming faded. Sue thought she heard a choked little gasp at the end, but that couldn't be possible. Couldn't have happened. No noise like that could come from the throat of so perfect a being. Even Sue's own breath was too loud in the silence.

Kara's voice startled Sue into opening her eyes again. "Now you understand."

"I don't belong here at all."

Kara reached out a hand to cup Sue's chin. The rich brown had drained from it, leaving the familiar dark gray, and a bright scar marred the back of it.

That, at least, was familiar. Those, at least, were flaws.

"I would not have brought you," Kara said, "if I didn't think you could belong."

"And I'm supposed to thank you? After you showed me… whatever that was? Made me feel like I don't even belong in the same galaxy as you, much less the same room?"

"I could have killed you, Sue Jones. Most of us would have. Your ship crashed. A perfect excuse, if any of us needed one."

Sue shivered. "And then?"

"That depends." Kara's grip tightened on Sue's chin. Sue froze, fearing the claws' prick. "Most of us wouldn't care, not after the intruder had been dealt with."

Dealt with.

"An Outcast like that would just leave your soul to wander," Kara finished.

That didn't sound good. "Just leave me down there?"

"Sift through your memories for sins enough to take you to the surface. Then do it. To them, it would be a novelty."

Sue shuddered. Kara let go of her chin and made a gesture of disgust.

"And you didn't. I get it. But then what was all that singing about?"

"You are a human. A mortal. I am—" Kara looked down at herself, at her gray skin, the network of cracks torn in it, "something beyond you."

Sue put a hand to her head. "That's why you think of me as a pet."

"That is why the others do."

"And that's what you want me to be."

Kara fixed Sue with a fiery gaze and swept it over her body in unmistakable appraisal. "Did you think I didn't enjoy what just passed between us?"

"You're saying that if I want to stay with you, if I want you to touch me, if I want what just passed between us to happen again, I have to accept that I'm a possession?" Sue put her hands on her hips, her meekness forgotten.

Kara growled. Her hands twitched, and Sue slid to the edge of the cot and glanced toward the exit.

But Kara only sighed. "If you want to walk among us, to see the Rings, to behold our world from the proper place above, rather than below—"

"I have to do it as your pet."

"Yes."

"Otherwise you'll kill me. Some choice."

The shadows around Kara stirred. "Otherwise the other Outcasts might try."

Chapter Eleven

Sue walked behind Kara, staying a careful pace behind. Ordinarily, she might have liked the view. As lurid as Kara's scar was and as much as her shadows hid, her back was shapely. So was her rear end.

But staring at a demon's cute ass didn't make up for trailing behind her like a slave or a toy. She looked down, her face hot with embarrassment. Her bad leg trailed behind her, and she knew she should focus on standing straighter, but this whole damned business of belonging to Kara made her so angry she couldn't bring herself to focus on it.

Which makes it easier to limp along behind her anyway. Sue chewed her lip in frustration. But there wasn't much she could do about it. Not if Kara was right.

The words rang in her head. *The other Outcasts might try.* She thought of their curious faces, their blazing eyes. Some had looked surprised, amused, entertained even. Others had been angry.

And they were staring at her now. They fixed her with the same gazes as before, some curious, some angry. As before, their phantom wings moved behind them, kaleidoscopes of energetic shadow. But now she noticed something else: just how many of them were looking at Kara. They stared at Sue, yes, but they also stared at Kara, their eyes wide with disbelief, amusement, or disgust.

Some looked from Kara to Sue and back again with knowing little grins, as if they knew something. Sue scowled, but given what had passed between her and Kara the other night, she guessed maybe they did.

Why save me, when everyone looks at me like that?

But at least Sue got to gawk at the shops again. And this time, Kara hadn't just dumped a bowl of Glowy Nutritious Drink in front of Sue. This time, she'd led her through the gawking crowds to one of the restaurants and sat down at one of the bars. Then, with an exaggerated imperious gesture and what Sue had come to recognize as a flap of phantom wings, she'd ordered Sue to sit beside her.

Sue had obeyed, of course. But not without a sideways little smirk. Scared as she was, if Kara was going to be that overdramatic, Sue was going to laugh at it when she could.

The bartender—or waitress, or vendor, or whatever the hell you called the giant demon who sold you breakfast—was tall, taller than Kara. Slim, straight horns rose high above her head. She leaned down to peer at Sue, her eyes such a pale yellow they glowed almost white.

Almost. Because whatever god or being had banished them wanted to keep white for itself. Sue couldn't help but feel angry about that, even though she probably wasn't supposed to.

She thought of the old churches with a pang. She'd never liked them before, but she would like them even less now. Listen to them talking about demons and soul-stealers wanting to drag you to hell and think *no, wait, that's not how it is, not really. They build cities, just like us.*

Whether the Outcasts were evil or not, she had a feeling being here had ruined all that for her forever.

If she ever got back home, anyway.

"So this is your human."

"Yes." Kara made sound deep in her throat. "Her name is Sue. And she is hungry. As am I."

The other Outcast inclined her head, pointing her horns at the floor in an appeasing gesture. "Of course, warrior. What would you like?"

Kara made another guttural sound. But this one wasn't threatening. *Must be the name of the food.* Sue chuckled, wondering if her throat could even make that noise.

Then she blinked. She'd understood everything else they'd said. Had they been speaking English? Or did they just have some mysterious way to make sure lesser creatures understood? If they did, this stuff didn't have a name in English, or Human, or whatever.

It made her think of old legends. Wasn't there some myth that said angels or immortals ate different food than humans did?

She didn't have time to wonder too much about it. The other Outcast was already talking to Kara again. "And for your creature?"

Creature. Sue lowered her head so the woman wouldn't see her getting angry. It would probably look deferential too. Which only made Sue madder, but would help.

Kara rescued her. "She tolerated—" Kara made another guttural sound Sue couldn't copy.

"Of course she did," the bartender said. She leaned over and sniffed at Sue, like Dehek had. "But she is not injured, or unwell. I know only a little about living humans. But I suspect one of them could tolerate something more interesting."

Sue's head snapped up. She didn't like the woman's tone at all. "It tasted good. And I'd crashed my ship. Kara was just trying to make sure I was all right."

"Of course, of course," the waitress repeated, with a little twist of her mouth. The line between her lips glowed with her inner light. "I'm sure Kara did everything possible to keep you comfortable, little one."

Sue knew Kara would growl before she heard it. Hell, she kind of wished she could make that noise herself. But it did make her curious. What did that mean? Did Kara do this kind of thing often? She'd said there were other souls, human souls, down on the planet below.

Had she ever…?

A dull sound snapped Sue out of her reverie. She looked up to see a black bowl in front of her, filled not with cool blue liquid but with something misty red. She leaned down to smell it. Probably a weird thing to do back home, but the demons sniffed everything, so why shouldn't she?

It smelled like spices, a whole rush of them, filling her nostrils all at once. Cinnamon, cardamom, pepper, and something fiercer that made her wrinkle her nose. She could have sworn she heard a pop, the kind that came from crackling fires, and when she closed her eyes she saw colors: white, red, orange, yellow.

Does this thing really smell like spices, or is that just all I can imagine it does?

When she opened her eyes again, Kara was watching her. "Is that wise, Saja?"

"It's just a human, Kara. It will be fine."

Just a human. Sue lifted the bowl to her lips, maybe out of defiance, maybe out of curiosity. She took a tiny sip, careful lest it sear her.

It pricked her tongue like pepper, little embers in her mouth. It filled her mouth with warmth, crackling and exciting. She put the bowl down, swallowed, waited for her mouth to clear, and nodded to Kara.

Kara smiled. "Well."

Sue hadn't realized how hungry she was. She'd liked the drink from before, cool, minty, and refreshing. But this tingled through her veins, intense and exciting.

Which might be a problem, but she wasn't sure how much she cared. Not with Kara there to watch over her. She glanced over at Kara and drank deeper, bracing for the burst of heat and grinning when it came.

Kara's voice was a low note, a soft and reassuring darkness against the blaze of light. "What makes you so interested in my human?"

"I heard from Dehek about your little scuffle the other day, and I wanted to see your little beast for myself."

Little beast. Was that what Kara thought of her? What her song was all about? Sue blinked, and a riot of color disappeared behind her eyes. The waitress seemed friendly enough, but she was still a demon. And Sue could only trust one of them.

Saja sniffed at Sue like Dehek had. She reached out narrow fingers with long claws and buried them in Sue's hair.

Sue froze, shocked fully awake now and not daring to move. *The other Outcasts might try.*

Kara growled. "That is mine."

Sue felt herself flush, but she couldn't tell whether she was feeling indignation or desire. Or even just the last aftertaste of the spicy drink. Who knew what fallen angels put in their food?

But the way Kara said those words, that growl in her hollow voice, a beast ready to rend and tear at any threat to her property…Sue felt the warmth pool in her sex, and cursed herself for a damn fool.

"I mean no disrespect, warrior. But what you have here is a living human." The claws curled against Sue's scalp and she winced, afraid of being pricked. "And her hair is a mess."

"What?" Sue wasn't sure if she'd said it or if Kara had.

"This creature isn't one of us, and you're not caring for it properly."

"Wait!" Somehow, as angry as Kara made Sue, hearing someone else talk like Kara didn't know what she was doing made her bristle.

Saja ignored her. "Look at its hair." She pinched at a lock of it, not gently, and held it up. "It's tangled and greasy."

Before Sue had a chance to react, she swiped out with her other hand. Sue saw light gleam on the claw as it swiped at her. She froze. But the claw only cut through the offending lock of hair and left it hanging in Saja's hand.

"Did you have to do that?"

But Saja ignored Sue and dropped the lock of hair in front of Kara on the table. "See? Oily and tangled." The hand still in Sue's hair pinched at her scalp.

Kara growled. Sue held still, but bit her lip in a small gesture of defiance. Fighting back might get her scalp torn up, but at least she could show Kara how it felt.

"You really should cut it off," Saja said. "Or at least learn to tend it. Have you never cared for a creature with fur before?"

Kara didn't answer her. Instead, she looked sidelong at Sue. "Have I neglected you?"

"Take your hands off me." Sue glared as best she could at Saja, emboldened now that she wasn't going to tear the rest of Sue's scalp out. "Then I'll tell you."

Saja ripped her hand away, not bothering to be gentle. The claws stung. Sue bit her lip, determined not to show either of them how fragile she was. Saja seemed friendly enough, but she had been talking to Dehek, after all.

Sue didn't look at Saja. Only at Kara. "She's right. It needs a good washing and combing. Your soap works well enough to wash it, but I need something to comb it with or it's just going to tangle." She cleared her throat. "Didn't you…did you have hair? Before, I mean."

"What?" Kara's voice was cold.

"I saw it, during the song. There was light. Shining around your heads."

Kara growled again, long and low and echoing.

"Warrior," Saja said.

Sensing Kara's tension, Sue took a quick sip of her food. The flavors seared her mouth and throat, but on their heels came the same heady crackle as before.

"You cannot hide what happened to us. Not even from your creature."

Kara opened her mouth, the light in her throat a furnace of flame, and let out a low, reverberating wail.

I'm here for you. It was a stupid thought, a foolish platitude. But at least it was honest. Sue slid her hand over Kara's.

Saja's eyes widened and she smirked. Sue glowered up at her, daring her to say something.

Kara lowered her head. She looked down at Sue's hand and her lips twisted into a wry smile. "Come. We are leaving." She shot a glance at Saja. "Add this to the credit I have with you."

So Saja was a friend. That was good to know.

Saja nodded. "Very well."

Kara was already walking away, her shadows a swirl behind her.

"I can tell you where you might purchase a comb for your pet's hair," Saja called from behind them.

CHAPTER TWELVE

Kara didn't take her back to her little room.

They walked through the marketplace, Sue making sure to keep behind Kara, despite her mounting frustration.

Some of the Outcasts watched them. As before, some looked curious, their bright eyes wide. Others looked angry. But they kept their distance from Kara, who strode past them, standing tall, as though daring any of them to challenge her.

No one did.

Sue looked up at Kara, at the scars that marred her back. She wondered, not for the first time, how Kara had gotten those scars. *She really is a warrior.* Not like Dehek, born with a vengeful being's curse. *Whatever she did in the war, she's someone they respect.*

Vengeful being. What did that mean? The old stories said the one who'd cursed them all was God Himself. That these people weren't just rebels, they were people who had chosen Evil.

And could never repent.

Sue shook her head. That didn't make sense. Kara had been kind. So had Saja and the other shopkeeper, even if they did call Sue an animal.

And the shops still dazzled her: restaurants and bars full of the strange liquid food. A bigger store she suspected was a grocery. Shops selling tiny computers, like the tablet she'd given up on. A big shop, the Ring around it built tall and wide to accommodate the showroom, selling vehicles, mostly small hovercars. Even a shop selling cloths. Sue convinced Kara to let her buy a few, though she wasn't entirely sure how to make clothes and sheets out of them. That was all right. She'd manage somehow.

They passed more groups of singers and minstrels, playing and singing their image-weaving songs. Apparently, Outcasts liked their music. And art, if the images counted as art. Sue guessed they did. They reminded her of paintings and dreams at the same time.

Some sang about the time before the Fall, some about the life they'd made for themselves here. They stopped in front of a group singing about the Rings and the Outcasts who built them, hovering on their shadowy wing-stumps for a few minutes at a time, building their new home panel by panel.

Sue smiled. There was something defiant about that. *Something brave. We've been sent to hell, but we'll make a home out of it anyway.* She grinned at one of the singers as he finished his song.

"Human," he said, his voice low and echoing. Kara made a noise of warning, but Sue didn't heed it. She'd need friends here if she wanted to do anything but shadow Kara and sneak off to have sex with her every now and then.

That didn't sound so bad, but it wasn't a life.

"Hi!" she tried. She thought, briefly, of calling him "Outcast," but it might bring up bad feelings. Especially since he'd sang about life here. The beauty of the Rings, the perseverance of the people.

"You enjoyed my song."

"Yeah. It was beautiful. And you're right. This is a nice place."

He smiled, his mouth too full of fangs. "As nice as one can find in exile."

What was she supposed to say to that?

He waved a hand. "If you're here, you too are far from where you belong."

Sue winced. "Well, I—"

"Easy, human. If you are in Kara's company, I welcome you. Strange as it is to see one of your kind here."

The other musicians nodded. Their wing shadows rustled around them.

"Welcome," echoed one of the women. "Though you have a great soldier watching over you right now. You are a lucky creature, human."

"Thank you," Sue said in as formal a tone as she could muster.

Kara nodded to them, a much smoother formal gesture. "I thank you for your esteem."

The demons waved their shadowy wing remnants in farewell.

It was a good sign. Apparently, not everyone here hated her after all.

Just most people.

The bustling marketplace, it seemed, had an end, and the Rings narrowed as they reached it. The noise and the bright lights faded, and the play of wing shadows gave way to harsh lights.

They stopped in front of a plain door, big and wide, sized for an Outcast but big even then. Glyphs decorated it, glowing green. Kara pressed a clawed hand to a panel and stared into a scanner, and they flared a brighter green.

Kara intoned something. Sue suspected it was less about opening the door and more for Sue to hear it. She hadn't learned many of the untranslatable words, but she thought she heard something about loyalty or perseverance.

"Welcome," said Kara, and gave what Sue suspected was an ironic little bow.

They stepped into a dim room, purple-tinted lights glowing from panels on the walls. A large screen filled one wall, almost like in the little room she'd come to consider hers, and a long sofa sat in front of it.

Upholstered with cloth, no less. Kara must have been someone important. Sue rushed toward it. It would feel so good to sit—or even to lie down!—on something soft.

"Eager, are you?" Kara teased her. Sue ignored her and flopped down onto the sofa.

After so long on her little cot, it felt like heaven.

"You like that?" Kara said. "Then come into the bedroom."

Sue grinned. *Don't mind if I do.* But she was tired of following Kara around like a lost puppy, and besides, she'd started all of this with an adventure. Might as well see what a demon's apartment looked like.

Luxurious one-bedroom, overlooking hell.

Off to one side Sue could see what she suspected was the equivalent of a kitchen, with a small table and some cabinets above it, bearing bowls and bottles of various sizes and shapes. Most looked empty, but dim light winked from a few.

I guess some ambrosia keeps. Sue chuckled. But beside the cabinet stood something mounted on the floor that might have been the alien equivalent of a refrigerator.

She made up her mind to raid it even as she followed Kara into the bedroom.

❖

The room turned out to be plain, dimly lit like the living quarters. Like them, it was lit by strips in the walls, glowing red and pink and purple.

The bed was big and looked comfortable, though to Sue's disappointment it was thin like the cot she'd lain on. Oh well. Kara was a soldier, after all.

At least it had sheets, or the equivalent, dyed dark colors but patterned with bold streaks of red and gold. Sue looked from the bed to Kara, whose scars glowed in the dim light.

It suited her, Sue decided.

Kara lay down on the bed and beckoned to Sue with one crooked claw. "Come here, pet."

Sue peeled off her clothes, but stayed put. "You like this too much."

"And you want to come and lie down with me."

"Well, yes."

"Then come." Kara drew back the sheet.

Sue climbed in and nestled against her. Her body was warm, her skin a strange but inviting texture.

"Let me touch you," Sue said. "I played your game all day. Now let me."

"Aren't you tired?"

"Yeah. But I want you."

"I want you too, human. Those hands of yours are soft, strange as they are."

Sue grinned. *So I did get through to you.* She slipped an arm around Kara, who shifted under her hand, obviously enjoying the touch.

"I would like to rest. Tomorrow."

Sue rolled her eyes, but didn't argue. Kara's warmth was already tugging her toward sleep. She wrapped her arm tighter around Kara's stomach and closed her eyes.

Chapter Thirteen

Sue stirred in her sleep. Images burst through her mind, violent as a sudden spray of blood.

First, a boy lying inert on the pavement of her colony at home. His hair was black, his eyebrows thick, his skin a shade darker than Sue's. Blood ran from his nose and over his cheeks, and his body jerked as someone kicked him. Jeers and laughs of encouragement rang out. Pins on his jacket glowed and flickered, but otherwise he didn't move.

Sue slipped forward as best she could. In the strange twisted time that came with dreams, she could still hear his cries even though he had stopped speaking, the lilt of another colony's accent in his pleading voice.

Now she rushed forward. She didn't have anything perfect to say, just "Stop!" "No!" "What do you think you're doing?" But she knew exactly how she wanted to say them: in the ringing tones of a soldier, a pilot, a woman with the authority to stop the mob in its tracks and turn away and find some other sport.

Only the words wouldn't come out. They stayed jammed tight inside her throat and choked her. She tried to speak, to spew them out, but they wouldn't come. She gaped instead. Like a fish. Like a person trying to breathe.

A person who would never speak at all.

One of the gang turned to her, a reveler's grin on his face. His lip twisted into a snarl as he stared at her, and he reached out pale hands.

She didn't stay. She didn't fight. She turned and ran.

Her bad leg was a dead weight behind her. Her heart hammered in her chest. She'd never make it. Never get away. She hadn't saved the boy, hadn't even tried. And now she'd never save herself.

She willed herself to run. She'd have to run faster than she ever had before, if she wanted to live. Red sand misted her vision and winds swirled around her, grit cutting at the skin of her face and neck. But the hands reaching for her from behind were gone, at least.

She wrapped her ruined jacket around her like a cloak from some old story, trying to protect herself from the bitter winds. They cut at her anyway, making her close her eyes.

People passed by, their heads down, their bodies wrapped in frayed clothes that could never protect them from the elements here. But they stood about as tall as Sue or only a little taller, and they had hair on their heads and no halo of shadow around them or bright cracks in their skin.

Humans!

"Hey!" Sue called out to one of them, a man. He lifted a weary head, cragged with wrinkles, and shook his head.

"Hey!" Sue tried again.

But his response was a mournful note, too deep for any man to make. Flames rose around him, fed by the winds. Close to him, too close, too close.

This is hell. This guy isn't a live human. He's a damned one.

And I'm here too, because I didn't save the boy. I'm here too, because I deserve to be.

As if in answer to her thoughts, Outcasts rose out of the mists, their bodies massive. Shadows swirled all around them, light blazing from the cracks in their stony flesh. They carried whips, glowing with the same energy as their bodies and their scars, and when they crashed down with them the winds followed, flame rising on their heels.

Like they weren't weather at all, but something made by the whips. One more thing to torture the damned souls.

Sue knew she should run. But her bad leg didn't want to move, emergency or no, and the glowing eyes of the Outcasts froze her where she stood. She stared at them, fixed in place, looking for anyone she knew, Kara or Saja or even Dehek, the angry child who'd taunted her so eagerly before.

Instead, a massive Outcast rose from the sands in front of her, his flint-gray torso spanning half the horizon, his horns spearing the roiling sky. His eyes and scars blazed orange, and the shadows that curled around him turned the red stormy sky black. One of his hands reached out for the humans, his claws the size of Sue's forearms. He clenched his fist around them and they disappeared. They faded, a gray mist torn asunder by his curling fingers.

Sue's ears filled with their wailing, with the winds that carried them away, and with the sounds of their dissolution.

Of course. They were dead. She was alive, and they were dead, and this was—

The Enemy. The real one, not the one the Outcasts gave that name.

Terror froze Sue in her place. *The Lord of the Outcasts.*

He raised his other arm, a fiery scourge held in his hand. The tails swung and winds came with them, knocking Sue to the ground. She clutched at the sand beneath her and stared up at him. His eyes blazed back, and Sue couldn't tell if he was looking at her or looking through her, looking past her, looking at the kinds of things only a fallen angel could see.

But he raised his whip, and it blazed with the fires of this strange new hell she'd found and brought it crashing down.

Sue thought of the boy. Had he lived? Had he died? Had they killed him once she'd left? She closed her eyes, his face still filling her mind's eye, and hoped she'd have enough strength not to scream.

❖

She awoke lying beside something warm, half like stone and half like flesh. The warmth felt good. She burrowed closer to it, hoping it might ease the hammering of her heart.

Her eyes were closed, but still she could see the boy's bloody face. She took deep breaths and opened her eyes.

Shadow curled around her, but in the midst of it, golden light blazed. Light and warmth and—

Kara.

I'm with Kara.

I'm safe here.

She wrapped an arm around Kara's body and clutched at her, willing herself to calm down.

Kara stirred beside her, the shadows moving. "Sue? What is it?"

"A dream," Sue said. "I had a dream. A bad one. Some memories. Memories I can't quite leave behind."

Kara stirred beside her. Sue pulled away just enough to let her turn and face her. Like her scars, her eyes were gold and bright.

"Some memories are difficult," Kara said after a long moment. She reached up to touch Sue's hair. "And the difficult ones are the ones that don't leave us."

CHAPTER FOURTEEN

"You fought a war," Sue said.

"And lost it," Kara said. She waved a hand. "And became this."

"What were you fighting for?"

Kara gave a guttural growl and shook her head. "We had always been favored. Always been honored above the other angels. We were the warriors. The defenders. The protectors of a world of light."

"Heaven." Sue closed her eyes and imagined it. A place filled with the souls of the dead, laughing and singing. A plain under an endless sunny sky.

The souls of the good dead, anyway. The boy's image burst across the backs of her eyelids again. Would she be one of those good dead? She didn't even know if he'd lived or died. She thought of the hand, in her dream, raising its fiery whip.

She almost felt like she deserved it.

"Heaven," Kara repeated, tasting the word.

Sue opened her eyes to banish the vision. To replace the terrifying Outcast in her mind with Kara, the one who made her feel good.

"Our stories say it's where the dead go. A place in the skies, as wide as space."

Kara's eyes widened. "Wide as space? It's just a world, like this one."

"Where the dead go."

"Nowadays, yes. Some human souls go there. But when we lived there, it was for us."

"Is that why you rebelled?"

Kara chuckled. "It's why some of us did. That was an age ago."

"I won't be offended." Sue grinned. "Well, not very. I don't like many humans either."

Kara's shadows settled around her. "Maybe that was part of it, for me. But that world was where we lived as we liked, and served only one."

"The one you rebelled against."

"Yes."

"We call him God. Or some of us do, anyway."

"He has great power, yes. Great enough to make worlds. Great enough to do this."

She sat up and stretched. The scars torn through her chest glowed in the dim light. Then she turned, twisting her body to expose the thick scars on her back. They glowed too, a sick malignancy, and Sue felt bile rise to the back of her throat. She swallowed it down, Kara's wing shadows swelling around her.

She couldn't help herself. She reached out and splayed her fingertips against the scar.

Kara growled a warning, but Sue didn't move her hand. She slid her fingers over the raised, textured skin, let her fingertips curl inward toward the glowing hollow in its center.

"You didn't deserve this," Sue whispered.

"What if I did?" Kara answered, still under Sue's hands. "I was a soldier. A rebel. A killer. And a traitor to the only empire I ever knew."

"No." Sue ran her hands over the scars again, slipped them over the rough stone of Kara's back. "No."

"I am a destroyer."

"You're more than that. Much more than that."

Kara said nothing.

"Turn around," Sue said. "So I can look at you. Not just at your scar."

Kara did. Sue looked her over, the tall horns curving from her head, the sculpted shape of her body, the bright fissures in her skin, the smooth delta between her legs.

Sue reached out and touched her shoulder, pressing her fingertips over one of the cracks. Sue closed her eyes and let it warm her. Let Kara feel her fingers, splayed against the stone of her skin. Then she slipped her hand down over Kara's breasts and moved them over the gray pebbles of her nipples.

Kara's eyes flickered and she let out a reverberating moan. Her fanged mouth parted and her throat was filled with fire. Sue's sex pulsed at the sight. She'd done that. She'd caused that. She'd made an Outcast feel that. She pressed her legs together, wanting the friction.

But this wasn't just about her. She moved her hand down over Kara's stomach, firm with something like muscle, even though there was only heat and energy beneath her skin.

Strength. Strength that even the Fall couldn't take away. She slid her hand over Kara's hip, the flesh under her hand hot with inner fire or lust or both.

She'd take either. "Lie down."

Kara tilted her head. "Now you're giving me orders?"

Sue just stared, willing herself to look commanding, like the soldier she'd always hoped to be.

Kara lay on her back and looked up at Sue with a comfortable, lazy smile. Sue slid her fingers down. Kara bucked to meet them.

Her labia were polished channels of worn stone. And they were warm under Sue's hands, too warm. But this was Kara, and Kara wouldn't hurt her.

She took a deep breath. The shock of heat became a steady hum under her fingertips.

It felt amazing.

She slid her fingers over the stony flesh for a long moment. Kara had called her hands soft, and she wanted Kara to feel that softness. To know just who and what was touching her.

Kara's eyes were glittering slits. She let Kara watch and wait a moment longer and then slipped her fingers over the nub of Kara's clit.

Kara's eyes opened and so did her mouth, a bright fanged grin. Sue moved her fingers, reverently at first. Then she sped up. Kara might be an immortal, but right now she was a woman, too. Someone to touch, to feel, to watch, to hear.

Kara panted and tilted her hips again. Sue slid her fingers down to Kara's entrance. There was wetness, a slow drip of thick fluid, a warm honeyed molasses.

Not like this, Kara had said. That was an understatement.

Like Kara's skin, her entrance was warm. Too warm for foolish and curious humans.

Sue didn't hesitate. She plunged her fingers in.

A ripple of heat shot through Sue's nerves, through her fingers, her palm, her wrist. For a moment, all she knew was that warmth, and she fell still, forgetting completely what she meant to do. But a growl of encouragement brought her back to herself.

Kara reached for her shoulders, her back, kneading lightly with clawed fingers. Sue grinned at the biting encouragement and began to move.

The warm core around her wasn't quite like a human's. Not as soft, not as flexible. But it pulsed around her, and she could lose herself in it just as easily. She moved her fingers again, thrusting in a steady rhythm. Kara trembled around her again and she sped up.

Kara threw back her head and moaned. She clutched at Sue's back, digging in. It stung, but Sue didn't mind. Kara had always touched her like she was something delicate. She could let go now.

Sue moved her thumb over Kara's clit, a wave of sympathetic desire building in her own sex when Kara bucked again, moving to her rhythm.

Come on. Come on. Be with me.

She leaned down over Kara and pressed her body to Kara's, skin to strange and burning skin. She pushed into Kara hard, thrilled her thumb against her clit as she pressed closer.

Kara wrapped a hand around the back of Sue's head and drew her into a fierce kiss. Her fangs worried Sue's lip, then bit, sending another little shock through Sue's nerves. Like the scratches, it felt good, a bright spike of intensity.

Kara took Sue's lip in her mouth and sucked at the wound. Sue moaned into her mouth and pushed into Kara harder.

Kara stopped, trembling under her hands. Sue pulled away from the kiss and laughed. *You're supposed to be the succubus.*

What would a succubus do? She pushed into Kara, teasingly at first, and then sped up. Kara roared, and tilted her hips again to match Sue's rhythm.

Sue moved her thumb again. Then she pulled her fingers out, leaving only her fingertips inside.

Kara growled something. Sue couldn't tell what. Maybe Sue's name. Maybe something in the language of demons. It didn't matter which. Sue drove her fingers in.

Kara opened her mouth and cried out. The hot core around Sue's fingers roiled, a little earthquake around her hand.

Sue pressed against Kara, feeling the solidness of her body beneath her and the warmth rising from her cracks, and slid her fingers free.

Kara slid her hands over Sue's back again, wrapped them around her, and tightened her grip.

❖

"Thank you," Sue said, still nestled against Kara.

"You wanted that badly to touch me, little human?"

Sue propped herself up on one elbow. "Of course."

"Very well." Kara's eyes were glittering slits in the dim light. "Now you have."

"But I don't just mean that. I mean…thank you. For letting me touch you. For letting me hear you."

Kara shook her head. Sue looked at her horns. They looked strange. Alien. And yet in spite of them, Kara could have been anyone else right now. Anyone who'd confessed something and was glad she did. "Our stories are not to be told. Or so it's said."

"By who? By the Enemy?"

Kara laughed. "Be careful, Sue Jones. You will start to sound like us if you talk like that."

"Maybe I don't mind sounding like you."

It wasn't completely true, of course. Not with the winds still howling outside, the red storms over a surface that Sue knew hid something terrible. Not with the dream she'd just awoken from. Not with whatever was down there still out there, and no one's word but a demon's that the humans trapped down there deserved whatever the hell it was they got.

But whatever war Kara had fought, whatever horrors she'd committed, whatever a demon still did—

"You have a story," Sue said.

"Of course."

"You have a story, and my people haven't heard it. They've heard—we've heard—something else. Something the people who told it wanted us to hear. Our priests. Or the angels. Or the gods, or whatever they were."

"We were never kind, Sue Jones. We made war and wanted to win it."

Sue closed her eyes. Her mind filled with the sounds of riots: fire, screaming, punching, kicking. Curses and insults, and if you were close enough, the sound of spittle flying. "You think that makes you different from humans?"

"Doesn't it? We punish you."

"You called it absolution before." Sue gave her a wry grin. "If it's absolution, then you know what some of us do to ourselves. To each other."

Kara growled. "Yes. I know what humans do. I know where humans come from, and I know what humans do."

"Then it's all the same. You're like us, and we're like you."

The shadows in the room danced. Kara's phantom wings settled over Sue, a heavy ghost of weight. "That was our fear."

"Your fear?" Sue froze. "You don't mean the rebellion was about us? About humans?"

"Part of it, yes. Our leader did not like the smell of these new, young beings that our lord had created. They stank of envy, of greed, of pettiness, of hatred."

"This was about us."

Kara's arms tightened around Sue. Sue tried to like it, to let it feel good. Protective. Comforting. But now she only felt afraid.

"This was about many things. Our leader is a prideful one. You will see it, when you meet him."

Sue shook her head. Meet the Devil? No, thanks. Not today. Not now. Probably not ever.

"He was already angry. Already discontent. So were the rest of us. We had always been precious. Favored. Elevated. Prized above all others."

Kara's wing shadows flickered again, snuffing out the light. "We knew, even before the humans were revealed to us, that something would change. Had changed already."

Her hand moved on Sue's back. "By the time he showed your people to us, we had already made up our minds."

"Then it wasn't us?"

A flare from Kara's fissures. "I thought it was, for a time. I probably thought it was even when I pulled you from your wreckage."

"But now you don't."

"Now I don't. The only thing seeing humans offered us was an excuse."

Chapter Fifteen

An excuse. To be demons.

And now here Sue was, a human, alone. A stranger. A member of the race that had started it all. She thought she'd made peace with it, but now her heart hammered in her chest. "When you pulled me from the wreckage?"

Kara's eyes narrowed to gleaming slits. "You did not belong here. Mortal or not, I know what it is to be stranded in a hostile place."

"The others didn't see it that way."

"The others didn't find your shuttle."

Sue let out a slow breath. "You saw me."

"I saw something, in the storm. I knew it looked unfamiliar. So I followed." Kara shook her head and chuckled. "Perhaps I am an explorer, like you. One needs it, to lead."

Sue froze under Kara's clawed hand. "To lead?"

Darkness flared out around Kara as her wing shadows shifted. "I was one of my lord's lieutenants. I was fighting for our people. Or so I believed."

"And how do you feel now?"

"I don't regret the rebellion. I don't regret our fight. It was a long time coming. But we were angry with our Enemy, and we should have focused on the ways he wronged us. Not on some new race of mortals who didn't even know themselves yet."

Sue stared around the room. She was here with Kara, safe, for the moment. Because she could be. Because it was safe to be with Kara in a way it never would with anyone else.

The room glowed and glistened around her. She was naked now, lying on something softer than her cot, with the one who'd touched her as intimately as anyone, here in a strange land.

"Thank you."

"Forgive me," Kara said, lowering her head. "Forgive us."

Me? On behalf of all the humans?

She reached out for Kara. Wrapped her hand around Kara's hairless head and drew it close.

"I'm not every human. I'm just a spacebus driver."

"You are Sue Jones. You are my human."

My human. It was still arrogant. Still rude. Still the kind of thing no being should say. But somehow, hearing it, Sue felt a tingle spread through her sex and a pulse of warmth deep in her chest.

She didn't know how she should talk about that. "And the others don't even know you're here. Not until they die."

"That is true."

"So I can't forgive you. Not for all of us." Kara's eyes flashed, and Sue traced her hand over Kara's neck. "But I can tell you one thing."

She pulled Kara in close, their mouths almost touching. "For me, there's nothing to forgive." She pressed her mouth to Kara's.

Kara's eyes widened. She opened her mouth and Sue slipped her tongue in. Her mouth and throat were warm, warm like the rest of her, and Sue clutched at the back of her head.

After a long, lingering moment, Kara broke the kiss. She drew away and looked at Sue, her head tilted, like she was curious.

"Thank you," she said, her voice such a low echo that Sue almost couldn't hear it.

❖

Kara held up the comb. It looked strange in her hand. A tiny trinket, too delicate, the kind of thing a warrior demon would crush if she even tried to hold it.

It fit the room, the glowing lights, the monitors, the cot, cleaner than anything Sue had ever lain on. But it didn't fit Kara's hand, a shape out of a tale, a legend.

That comforted her. This impossible being, awesomely powerful, holding a comb for her. It meant that even in this strange world, here in this place, she was safe. Safe as she'd ever be.

"Human," Kara said. "Sue."

Sue looked sidelong at her. "Yeah."

"This is for you. You know that, am I right?"

"Yes. Yes, I do."

Kara reached out and buried a clawed hand in Sue's hair. "Then let me."

"You want to brush my hair." Like a thing. Like a toy. Like the pet Sue was pretending to be.

And yet the look in Kara's eyes was earnest.

"I thought I would cut it first. So that it doesn't tangle."

"I don't see scissors."

Kara clicked her claws together.

Sue's eyes widened. "You can't be serious."

Kara grinned, all fangs. She laid her hand on Sue's head like Saja had, forceful and possessive. Sue froze under her hand.

"Why not? Saja did it. Why shouldn't I?" She curled her fingers inward, tightening her grip on Sue's hair.

Sue squirmed, an effervescent sensation making her twitch. She couldn't blame it on the hot meal. Not this long after it. "I don't want you to," she forced herself to say.

"Is that so?"

"You've got claws. You won't cut it evenly."

"No." Kara chuckled. "I won't. But who are you trying to impress? The only other humans here are on the surface. And I'm sure they don't care much about your fur."

"Hair."

"Hair, then." Kara relaxed her grip and tightened it again.

She's playing, Sue realized.

"Whatever you call it, understand this: People who have already made up their mind to despise you will do it no matter how well you are groomed." Kara's wing shadows moved, a sigh under her words.

Sue swallowed hard. What did she really want? For Kara to go hunting for a pair of scissors, somewhere in a marketplace neither of them belonged in? As normal as the room looked, she was in a demon's lair.

"All right," she said.

Kara slid her fingers over Sue's scalp, careful not to prick. One pushed against a knot in her hair, and Kara pulled her hand away.

She grabbed at a lock of hair and tugged, just tightly enough for Sue to notice the sting. Then her clawed hand reached out to snip through it. Sue watched it fall, a dark knot, ragged-edged and lonely against the pristine floor.

Cut by Kara's hands. Hands she'd only imagined from stories. Powerful, dangerous hands—that meant her no harm.

That sent a new spike of warmth through her. She was here, in her room, the place set aside for her. Protected by someone who'd been an angel a long time ago.

Kara rumbled, and Sue felt it in her sex. She shifted her hips, but didn't want relief. Not really. This was its own strange intimacy. Too much desire would just distract her.

So she breathed in and out and let herself feel it all. Kara's fingers, wrapping around a lock of hair and tugging it taut. The expectation and the faint thrill, something like excitement and something like fear, knowing a monster's clawed fingers were coming for her. The claw cutting through her hair. The tension releasing. Over and over, again and again, like the rise and fall of breath or tide.

She didn't belong here, not really. But for the moment, it was enough. She closed her eyes.

When Kara stopped, it felt like silence. A strange pause, a lull in a familiar rhythm. She opened her eyes and looked at Kara, who held up the comb.

Sue looked at it a moment, then turned her head to look into the mirror. Dark hair framed her face in an uneven bob, its edges jagged. Ugly and crude, and her hair was still full of tangles. But somehow it felt right, next to her torn clothes. Next to the fact she only had one set of clothes. It made her look strong, somehow. Defiant. A stranger in a land too big for her, facing it all anyway, her hair shorn by a demon's claws.

She grinned at her reflection. Kara's reflection grinned too, a thin line of light where her lips parted. She lowered the comb to Sue's scalp.

Her touch was confident, the easy grace of a warrior. But she didn't move the comb, just left it there, like she was thinking.

"You won't hurt me." Sue laughed. *And if you do, it's all part of the bargain. I'm mortal, and you're Something Else.*

Kara dragged the comb down. Too forcefully, and Sue let out a hiss. But it wasn't too bad. Kara didn't know her own strength.

That sent a thrill through Sue even as she winced. And Kara slowed down, pulling the comb through Sue's hair with exaggerated gentleness, the comb pinched between her clawed fingers like something delicate and precious.

I'm fine. I'm not made of glass. Sue didn't say it aloud. Kara was learning Sue's limits, learning her body. Better to let her do that herself than try to tell her everything.

And there was something about the way Kara treated her. Like she was something precious, something a mighty warrior was afraid to break. Maybe being a pet wasn't all bad.

The comb snagged on a tangle, and Kara pulled, making that long low sound that meant she was thinking or concentrating. It stung, but it wasn't too bad. Sue sucked in a breath and let it out again when the comb finally pushed through the knot.

Sue let her eyes droop but didn't close them. Not like she had before. Part of her wanted to lose herself, but part of her wanted to watch. To see Kara untangle the knots. To watch herself become clean again.

Kara worked out the knots and the stinging faded to a tingle in her scalp. She breathed deeply again, gave herself over to the rhythm again. Felt something stir inside her again, an effervescent crackle.

Kara laid the comb down. She looked at her reflection and Sue's in the mirror and then reached her hand out to touch Sue's hair. She ran her fingers through it, the claws just touching Sue's scalp. "Is that better?"

Sue smiled. "Yes."

"Have I done it correctly?"

"Almost."

Kara frowned.

"Don't worry about it. It's fine. I'm sure I look better than the dead ones."

"Yes." Kara ran her hand through Sue's hair again. Her hand was warm and felt good against Sue's scalp. And Kara grinned too. Like she liked the feeling.

Chapter Sixteen

Warmth spread under Sue's skin, but under it all she felt a pang. The dead ones. Whatever happened up here in the Rings, they were still down there. Someday, she'd have to face it. See what the Outcasts did to them. What some of them might do to her if they had the chance. Find out what was really happening here.

Kara's hand moved in her hair again. Sue sighed. Best to give in to it, for now. For now, she belonged to Kara, and she would let herself enjoy it.

Kara patted her again, and then slid her hand down Sue's cheek and ran a claw over Sue's lips.

Oh. Okay, if that's what you want. Sue kissed Kara's fingertip and opened her mouth. The clawed finger slipped into her mouth. She closed her lips around it carefully and sucked at Kara's fingers.

"Lie down, pet," Kara said and slid her fingers free.

Sue quirked an eyebrow at Kara but obeyed. Kara hovered over her, looking down at her with hungry eyes, and Sue's sex pulsed, already eager.

Kara leaned down and ran her hands over Sue's body. Her fingers moved down Sue's sides, the tips of her claws a gentle tickle, their sharpness a whisper of danger that made Sue gasp and fight to keep from twitching under Kara's hands.

Kara curled her hands inward, the claw tips pricking at Sue's sides. Sue took a shaky breath, trying to keep still, but her hips bucked anyway. Kara laughed and dug in, just enough to prick. Then she flattened her fingertips against Sue's skin and moved her hands down. Sue spread her legs, waiting.

But Kara didn't stop at Sue's hips or move to her vulva. Instead, she traced her way down Sue's legs. She paused at Sue's scar and traced her fingers over it, just as Sue had traced the scars where her wings had been.

"You don't need to—" Sue began.

"Shh." Kara cut her off, massaging the scarred skin and the muscles beneath.

Sue sucked in a breath. The scar ached, the skin and muscle hard and twisted. But it would loosen up if she let Kara work at it. And it had been a very long time since someone had bothered to try.

Sue smiled. The last one to try had been an old boyfriend. Sue wasn't sure she'd really loved him, but she'd liked his smile and she'd loved his hands. He'd always touched her with care, tending to her old hurts. But she'd always wondered, deep down, if she liked his touch or his reassurance. He'd been there after the boy, holding her, talking to her, trying his best to put her back together with his hands, his kiss, his flesh inside her.

She'd loved the first and needed the second and been less than sure about the third. It felt nice enough, his hips crashing against hers as he drove in and in and in. But her mind had always wandered, even as she spasmed around him and cried out his name. She found herself thinking of women. Soft hair and skin, firm breasts, slick vulvas. And a vague sense of guilt and sadness, knowing he was with her and she wasn't with him, not like she should have been.

This was different. Every time Kara's hands moved on her, little tingles thrilled through her. And Kara's hands were finding her hurt, pressing in, pushing until the hard knots gave. Making her wince only to sigh with relief as the muscle relaxed.

She stared up into the granite face. "Kara. Please."

Kara's hands slid over the scar and then let go. She chuckled and knelt at the foot of the bed, lowering her head down between Sue's legs.

All right then. Sue reached to wrap her hand around the back of Kara's head.

Kara kissed the soft skin of Sue's thigh. Then she opened her mouth, hot with the furnace of her inner fire. Sue moaned and stirred against her.

Then she felt fangs against her skin. Sharp, like the claws. She trembled once and stilled. Kara lingered there, pressing in just enough not to prick her.

"Go ahead," Sue murmured, locking her hand around Kara's head.

Kara looked up at her. "You want this?"

"You're a warrior. My warrior. You have claws and fangs. That's who you are. What you are. I want it all."

"Very well."

Kara kissed her thigh again. Sue closed her eyes. Then the fangs sank into her flesh.

Pain burst through Sue's nerves, a sudden shock of sensation. She felt the warmth of her own blood, dripping down where Kara pierced her. All her awareness focused on Kara, on what Kara had done and was doing to her. It scoured away the discomfort, leaving only a searing prick of desire.

Kara growled and pressed her lips to the wound. Then she opened her mouth and licked away the blood she'd drawn and lapped at the wound. It felt soothing, drowsy, intoxicating, the gentleness a balm.

Yes. Yes. I want this. I want it all. Sue didn't say it. All she did was mewl and pant and lock her hand even tighter around Kara's head.

Kara licked at the wound one last time. Her lips ghosted along the flesh of Kara's thigh. "So soft," she purred against Sue's skin.

She traced her way up to Sue's vulva. Sue moaned again and spread her legs.

Clawed fingers spread Sue's inner labia apart. Sue didn't bother keeping still. Dangerous as Kara was, Sue knew her now. Knew she had nothing to fear.

Kara sniffed at Sue's wetness, like the other Outcasts had sniffed at Sue before. But they'd been scenting a stranger. They'd been suspicious. This was Kara, taking her in, discovering her with all her senses.

"Please," Sue whispered.

Kara pressed her mouth against Sue's skin. She parted her lips, and Sue could feel her inner heat. She bucked her hips, hard, and Kara gripped her hips, holding her in place.

The power in Kara's grip sent another tingle through Sue's flesh. *If this is what it means to be your pet, I guess I can get used to it.*

Then Kara began to lick, laving Sue's clit with slow, methodical strokes.

Sue wrapped her other hand around Kara's head, pressing it as hard as she could into her flesh. Kara laughed against her skin and sped up, matching Sue's frantic movements.

Then she moved off Sue's clit and slipped her tongue inside.

Sue snarled, half wanting Kara to keep lapping at her clit, half welcoming her Outcast inside her. She gasped and panted as Kara's tongue moved inside her.

Kara slipped free of her again. She took one of Sue's inner lips into her mouth, sucking at it, and then taking it between her fangs. They pressed against the flesh, sharp but not piercing. Sue froze, a frisson of fear only heightening her desire.

Kara wouldn't hurt her, but Kara was a living weapon. Sue panted, wanting.

Kara opened her mouth again. She moved to murmur against Sue's clit, a humming vibration.

"Please," Sue said again. She would have said it loudly, but only managed a needy little gasp.

Kara snickered against her flesh and flicked her tongue over Sue's clit. Sue bucked against her lips matching her rhythm.

Her flesh locked and she pushed out her hips, grinding hard against Kara's lips and tongue as she let out a long, high cry.

CHAPTER SEVENTEEN

"I have to see the dead ones."

Kara turned away from the mirror and stared at Sue, her eyes wide. "The dead ones?"

"Yes." Sue nodded, trying to look as decisive as the pilot she'd once hoped to become. "The ones your people punish. They're humans. Like me. I have to know what it's like for them."

Kara stepped closer. "Those humans aren't like you, Sue Jones. They are the worst of your kind. Rapists. Murderers. War criminals."

Sue shuddered. If she went down there, if she met those other humans, she'd be right next to horrible people. Whether there were Outcasts around to punish them or not.

"Then most humans don't end up here," she said, choosing her words carefully.

"No."

"Then it's not 'accept me or else.'"

"What?"

"That's how the old religion tells it. That you either accept God—the guy you Outcasts call the Enemy—or else you go to hell." Sue swept a hand out in front of herself. "Which is here."

Kara laughed and moved to sit on the cot next to Sue. "That's not exactly it. Though perhaps the Enemy would like it to be." She sighed. "We have not heard from him in what you humans would consider an age. Maybe several of them. We only know the task we were given, and the ones who come here so that we can perform it."

Sue's eyes widened. "He left you alone, then?"

"Once he banished us, yes. And gave us the duty to punish those humans who came to us for absolution."

"Wait. Who came to you for absolution?"

Kara nodded.

"You mean these…you mean the people in hell want to be there?"

"Want to be in hell?" Kara chuckled again. "Very few want that." Sue turned to her and held up a finger. "But every soul knows what it has done. And those that have done terrible things cry out for absolution. We give it to them."

Sue's brow furrowed. "Their souls cry out? Does that mean they want it, or does that mean they don't?"

"It means they know what they have done, and they know what they deserve." Kara reached out to touch Sue's cheek.

Sue flinched. "They want you to torture them?"

"They tell us. They submit." Kara's fingers hovered inches from Sue's skin, but she made no attempt to touch Sue again.

They know what they deserve.

The boy. His jacket. His blood spattered face, his brown skin. His dark hair.

"I've done things too," Sue whispered.

Kara's hand settled against her chin, a gentle touch. "No one is innocent."

Sue blinked. "What?"

"None of us is pure. None of us is perfect. We all carry memories. We all carry hurts."

Tears welled up behind Sue's eyes. "I couldn't save him."

Kara looked at her. Her eyes flickered with some emotion Sue couldn't read. "I'm certain you tried," she said at last.

"That's just it!" Sue cried. Her tears became hot pricks of anger, and she let them fall. "It's not just that I didn't save him. It's that I didn't even try."

"I'm sure that you attempted it. I know you."

"No." Sue grabbed at Kara's arm and wrenched it away, surprising herself with her own strength. From the way Kara's lips pursed, she'd surprised Kara too. "That's what I'm trying to tell you. I didn't try."

Kara didn't say anything. Sue gulped in air and spoke again, tears blurring her vision. "There are a lot of riots in the colonies. The cities aren't even cities. Not really. Just a bunch of buildings people live in. Try to work in. Some are factories. Some program the robots that make things in the factories. Doesn't really matter. There's not much to do anywhere, except push people around and get in trouble. And protest the city councils. Kick that one out, bring that one in. Do the whole thing again six months later."

She laughed. "People are afraid of the cops. When they put down riots. Which is only sometimes. Everything's crazy. I wanted to be a starfighter pilot, because they…they're what people who protect people should be. They see the whole galaxy, go out among the stars. They know better than just to push around some crowd that pushes back and kills them too."

"Go on."

Sue shrugged. "Then there's me. I drive a spacebus. Take people from one end of—well, I would have said hell, but there's a whole other definition of that around here—to the other."

Kara lowered her head. "Hell is a place of punishment, Sue. There are many of those, spread out among the galaxies and hidden between worlds."

"Yeah, I'm sure there are," Sue quipped. Her heart pulsed heavy in her chest.

"You're not getting out of this that easily." Kara's lips curled into a wry smile. "Finish your story."

"There was a riot," Sue began, swallowing hard. "Two groups, back and forth, yelling about some man or other on some city council. I didn't hate him. This kid didn't either. But the people who did found him. Saw his pins flashing political slogans."

"So they attacked him," Kara finished for her.

"Yeah."

"And you couldn't stop them."

"I didn't even try. I wanted to. I wanted…I wanted to be like one of the pilots. Not just a bus driver. Someone trained. Someone powerful. Someone who puts her life on the line to save people." She licked her lips.

"And you didn't intervene."

"I knew what I wanted to say. What I wanted to do. What I was gonna do. I was going to rush in and tell them to stop it, tell them no. Tell them in two months it would be the other way around, one of them down on the ground, begging and pleading and blood coming from his nose and mouth—"

"Shh," Kara soothed her and leaned in closer.

"But the words got stuck. Caught in my throat. I said something. Just some noise that didn't mean anything."

"You tried."

"They heard me and turned around. I just ran." She glared down at her leg. "My leg felt like a stone. I couldn't get away fast enough. Someone grabbed my jacket. I felt hands—" She shuddered and stopped.

"But you got away." Kara slid her hand to Sue's shoulder.

Sue glared back at her. "I ran and ran. I got away. But here's the question: Did I deserve to?"

"No one is innocent," Kara repeated. "Think of Dehek and the scars on his back."

"Dehek didn't deserve that!"

"He would kill you if he had the chance, Sue. Now you defend him?"

Sue blinked. "What are you getting at? Are you saying Dehek deserved to be born without his wings?"

"No, Sue. I am not."

"Dehek wasn't born evil. No one is."

"Some are, perhaps. I do not know. But you're right. The Enemy is wrong to curse us all from the beginning." She traced a hand over Sue's chest. "As you are wrong to curse yourself."

Sue hung her head. "All I needed to do was say something. And I couldn't even try."

"You were at risk. You might have incited them against you."

"So?"

"There is a difference between heroism and foolishness, Sue." Kara's hand moved on Sue's shoulder, in a soothing rhythm.

Sue wanted to give in to it, but she couldn't. "You're a warrior. How can you say that?"

"My people were trained for war. Long before we rebelled."

"Yeah. And you fought the war. Even though you knew that you might lose it."

"That is true. But violence is not something to risk lightly. And"—Kara pointed with her other hand, at the pale scar on Sue's leg—"you're fragile. Even for a human."

Sue clenched a fist. Tears pricked at her eyes again. "I don't even know if he lived or died! I just know that he went still."

Kara answered with a mournful note, like part of a chant or a song. A wisp of vision came with it, a black cold cot in an empty room. A woman's shape, hunched over, her horned head held in clawed hands. A mist of shadow danced grief around her.

And beneath the shadow, her back was scored with blazing scars the darkness could only dim so much.

The vision was bad enough, but the humming note was worse, a current of mourning that Sue couldn't will away.

Is that how it was? After your war? Or are you just showing me you've been hurt too?

"You do not need absolution," Kara said at last. "Not for that. You're no warmonger, Sue Jones." She leaned closer, her face inches from Sue's, as if she wanted to kiss her.

Sue shook her head. "Maybe I don't. But if there are humans down there, I have to see them. They're like me. I have to know what's happening to them."

"Those humans are the worst of your kind." Kara gripped at her shoulder, too hard. Her eyes smoldered with anger.

But Sue knew, somehow, that Kara's anger wasn't aimed at her. "That doesn't matter."

"Very well," Kara sighed. "I will take you down there, if you're so certain that is what you need."

Chapter Eighteen

Kara didn't use Sue's shuttle.

Sue wasn't sure why she'd hoped Kara would. But she'd imagined it, the old weather-beaten hull of an old friend she barely fit in, cozy in the way only an old jalopy could be. And here on a faraway planet—if this was a planet, and not something weirder like a whole other dimension—it would've been a little piece of home. Sue sighed. Even the weird old rusty smells would comfort her right now.

And she could use some comfort. She only wanted to do this because not doing it felt wrong.

Kara's craft was too pretty. Not pristine, not like the homes and shops up above in the Rings. Sue had seen the scratches and pits in the hull when she'd climbed in, evidence of what sandstorms and lightning and flame could do, even to craft built by fallen angels.

And there were other ships here too, swooping in and out of the paths of the storms and the striking lightning. Sue couldn't see much through the storm, but what she could see looked as battered as Kara's craft.

But like everything else here, the ships were elegant. Finely crafted. A sleek, compact triangle that could weave between the paths of the buffeting winds. And practical as they were, the Outcasts couldn't resist embellishing them, it seemed. Designs curled around the hulls, mimicking twisting knots. Like whoever had built them took a little too much inspiration from the Rings that they called home.

The Outcasts liked their handiwork, it seemed. Just like their songs and their bowls of food. Sue knew the Outcasts had been warriors, but what about artisans? Maybe, when they'd taken up their arms, heaven had lost a few craftsmen.

Their craft dove toward the ground, pushing against the winds. Sue watched readouts flash across the window, on the sides and the top and the bottom. She still couldn't read the Outcasts' glyphs, but watching Kara's screen made her hands itch to touch the controls, to fly something. Her shuttle. Her spacebus back home. The starfighter she would never pilot. She flexed her hands and balled them into fists to ward off the impulse.

Their craft settled into a hover, just above the ground. "Look," Kara said and pointed.

Long rows of humans shuffled over the sands, their steps heavy. Lightning crackled near them. Flame rose from their feet as they passed. It caught on their garments and set the fabric ablaze. Sue cringed. But the humans didn't react to the fire rising around them at all. They walked through it and past it like they didn't know that it was there.

They acted entirely too normal to be on fire.

But they also looked drained. Colorless. Washed out somehow, all but the fire around them. White-skinned people looked an ashen beige, and brown and black people's skin looked wrong too, drained to dull, grayish shades. And their billowing clothes flickered, vanishing as if behind the clouds, and appearing again.

It was hard to see anything past the line of humans, but Sue could see some of the other Outcasts' ships. Some hovered above the humans, while others landed in the sands. And something else, rising in the distance. A tower, an obelisk, something. Glyphs glowed on it, a bright eldritch purple.

Don't go there! something inside Sue said. But the humans continued their march toward it, heedless of her little craft and surely unaware of her fear. Were they even aware that Sue and Kara were there?

They had to be. If they'd done unforgivable things and were being punished for it, they couldn't just be…empty. That would defeat the whole purpose.

"Look," Kara said again. She flicked her fingers over the controls, magnifying the view out the window until the humans' faces filled the display.

Their colorless clothes and skin were eerie enough, especially against the fire. But their eyes were even worse. Kara made sure Sue could see them. The dead humans' eyes had no pupils. And the irises had no color of their own either, dull and empty hazel swirling from blue to dirty brown and back again.

Do they even remember who they are? Or is all that's left what they did?

Sue cried out, a wordless noise she'd never made before. Would never have imagined herself making, not even during the riots back home. An empty, eerie sound, like the kind she imagined these dead would make if they weren't so calm.

Kara, merciful for the moment, ran her hands over the controls. The magnification faded, and with it those empty eyes.

But the sights weren't over. One by one, the humans stopped walking and stood in the pyres they'd made for themselves. They lifted both hands over their heads and clasped them together.

Sue looked at them, a chill seizing her. "What does that mean? What are they doing with their hands?"

"You wanted to see them," Kara said. "Now you have. If you wish, we can still turn back."

Sue swallowed hard. "No. I have to know."

"Then watch."

Sue let herself blink and then forced her eyes open. She'd asked for this. She'd chosen this.

Outcasts emerged from one of the ships that had landed. They didn't step onto the sands, but hovered, mantles of shadow spread out behind them.

They dove down toward the humans and landed near the ones who'd clasped their hands over their heads. The humans bowed their heads.

Absolution, Kara had said. These humans wanted it. Or agreed to it, at least. Did you go to hell because you thought you deserved it, or because someone else decided you did?

Like the Outcast in Sue's dream, some carried scourges. Others held other weapons, blades and knives and curling things Sue couldn't recognize. Mercifully, they weren't on fire. But they caught the light and held it.

When they struck out at the humans, the flames around the humans flickered and the clothes the humans wore vanished, as though the cloth and the fire alike had only been illusions.

Which they probably are. These people are dead, after all. Sue winced, staring at the too-exposed back of a pale-skinned man.

A blade tore into his back, wielded by a male Outcast who hovered just behind him. The human shuddered, a violent tremor wracking his body. He opened his mouth and let out a cry, a cry like the one that the sight had torn from Sue earlier.

Sue gasped and covered her eyes. The blade left no mark on the man's flesh, no bloodied slash leaking crimson. Instead, it ripped through his body itself. Where it had passed, Sue could see red.

Not the red of the man's blood, but the red of the sands beyond him.

He raised his head and cried out, his mouth open wide. The Outcast struck out at him again, the slashes erasing another part of him. The fire vanished too, and Sue winced. The "lake of fire" in the old religious stories was nothing. Not compared to this.

"They're destroying them," Sue whispered.

"No," Kara said. "One cannot destroy a soul."

The Outcast stopped. The man stood for a long moment, his back shot through with void, the winds moving through him. Then he began to walk, his movements slow and laborious, as he fought against the wind. Where he passed, embers glowed. The Outcast behind him followed with slow flaps of his wing shadows.

"What happens now?" asked Sue.

The humans stopped again. Sue closed her eyes. She'd seen enough.

"They march on. Toward the obelisk."

"And what happens to them there?"

Kara shook her head. "I will not take you inside."

Dread crept through Sue again, freezing her veins. "More of the same?"

Kara nodded. "Yes. More of the same. Only—"

"Only worse. I get it. But what about after that? What happens when they're done being punished?" Sue shivered. The old religion had said you burned forever. Was that what happened to these people? Over and over and over again?

Kara said nothing.

"What happens after?"

"That is not our concern."

"Kara—"

Kara sighed and held up a hand for silence. "I mean only that it depends on the will of the One." She growled. "A will we do not know, and have no reason to trust."

"But…" Sue trailed off. She couldn't bring herself to keep pushing.

"Humans were always beloved by the One," Kara said after a moment.

That wasn't an answer. But it would have to be enough. "And there are a lot of these things?" Sue pointed at one of the obelisks. "These towers, or whatever they are? Where your people punish the damned?"

Kara nodded again. "There are many on the surface. That was our task: to maintain them. To mete out the punishment the humans have earned."

"Your task?"

"That is what all Outcasts were given to do when we were banished here."

"All of you?"

"Yes."

Sue stared at Kara, at the strange woman with the stone skin, the horns, the claws, the fangs, the fiery eyes and glowing scars. She'd grown used to her, used to it all. She'd liked it, even. A monster for a bodyguard and a titan for a bedmate.

That was fine. That was all fine. But this? She should have known it, should have guessed it. Or maybe she had guessed it and just hadn't wanted to think about it, not when Kara's scars looked like gold and her claws felt like freedom.

What did those claws feel like to the people she was supposed to use them on? Sue bit her lip hard enough to hurt, then opened her mouth and exhaled. "All the Outcasts punish humans. Even you."

"Yes," Kara said again and lowered her head. "Even me."

CHAPTER NINETEEN

"Take me home," Sue said. "Now."

"Very well." Kara tapped at the controls again and their craft zoomed into the air, too fast. Like Kara wanted to get out of here as badly as Sue did.

They rocketed toward a bay in one of the outer Rings. As before, Sue stared at the controls, the readouts, the scrolling glyphs. But before, she'd felt a pilot's yearning. Now, she forced herself to focus on them, trying to ground herself. *I'm a pilot. Even if all I do is fly a bus.*

She took deep breaths, willing away what she'd seen and heard. Even after their craft had docked, she kept it up, inhaling and exhaling as slowly as she could.

Kara walked in front of her as always, a tantalizing shadow. But every time she looked over at the sway of her hips, she also saw a pair of milky, hazel eyes.

The door of Kara's apartment opened. Sue walked in, her steps robotic. "Leave," she said.

"This place is my home."

"I need to be alone. I need to think about what I saw down there." *I need to be away from you.*

Kara looked away. "I should never have showed them to you."

"That isn't the problem."

Except that it was. Except that now her mind filled with images of a still and bleeding boy, the dark eyes she remembered replaced with the blank, shifting eyes of the damned.

"Please, just leave me alone, Kara. Leave me be. This is about me and my people. Not you."

"Sue, I can't do that. I chose to protect you." She looked down. "And I failed. I can't leave you alone now."

"I'm stranded here, Kara. Stuck. In a place where my people are doomed. Are tortured." The words poured out of Sue before she could stop them. "The last thing I want right now is to be around one of the people who does it!"

"We didn't choose that. It was a decree."

"But you obeyed it. Your people did it. You did it."

"I've done many things, Sue Jones. Some of them I regret." She looked down. "Like this one."

Anger flared through Sue. She put her hands on her hips, knew she must look ridiculous, wasn't sure she cared. "You don't regret war."

Kara's head snapped up. Fiery light blazed between her clenched fangs. "I don't regret fighting for my people. I don't regret protecting them, as I tried to protect you. But I do regret war."

Protecting them? Sue knew Kara wanted to protect her, like Sue might protect a dog or cat or exotic creature from one of the colonies. But what was this? "That's not what you said to me before."

"You're right. It isn't. But it's true, all the same."

Sue hung her head. What could she say to that? And yet…

And yet she glanced over at Kara's hands and imagined them wrapped around the handle of a whip. A whip that tore people away. A whip that erased them.

"I need time," Sue said. "Time to think. Time to rest."

Kara huffed. "Very well." She looked around. "Would you like the bedroom to yourself?"

Sue shook her head. She wouldn't be getting much sleep tonight, not with those eyes boring into her every time she tried to close her eyes.

You should let Kara stay with you. Just for that, if nothing else.

"Go ahead," Kara said. "Sleep inside. I can rest here."

Sue shook her head again, violently this time. "The couch in here is fine."

Kara sighed. "Very well," she said again. She strode over to the door without sparing another look at Sue.

But when the doors slid open, she turned back. "You'll find the blue foodstuff in the cooling cupboard. It might soothe you."

"Thanks," Sue returned, her voice flat.

❖

Just like she expected, Sue didn't sleep. She stayed awake, her heart beating too fast, her eyes staring at the light panels in the ceiling. She tried to study them, count them, catalog their patterns. But blood and eyes and still faces kept invading her vision. Her bad leg throbbed.

Worse even than the jumble of memories was Kara's face, floating among them. In Sue's mind's eye, Kara tilted her head back and laughed, a horrible cackle from a burning throat.

They're demons. They torture humans. It's what they do.

What exactly were you expecting?

Sue tossed and turned on the little cot. Her stomach growled. She hadn't looked in the fridge—*cooling cupboard*, some part of her mind reminded her, a part that sounded a lot like Kara—for the bowl of blue liquid, even though she felt hungry for it.

It's what they do. And Kara does it too.

And yet Kara had wanted to protect her. Had talked like the war was about protecting the other Outcasts.

Thinking about that was the worst part. She missed Kara. She wanted Kara with her now.

She slid a hand down her inner thigh, looking for the spot where Kara had bit her. The skin felt soft, too soft, too vulnerable.

She slipped her hand over the mark, the grooved scab rough under her fingers. A day ago, she'd welcomed it, a fierce warrior's mark on her flesh. Now it seemed harsh, violent. The mark of a cruel creature, the kind that wouldn't change.

That's not fair. You told her you forgave her.

And Sue had touched her, too. She held out her hand and looked at it, remembering the thick ambrosia of Kara's wetness. Kara had trusted Sue. Had let Sue inside her. A mere mortal she'd called a pet.

Sue remembered the warmth, the eagerness. The flesh, not as soft as a human's, but open, warm, inviting.

The fangs, nibbling at her lip. Breaking the skin, in a burst of sensation that had stung but hadn't hurt.

It had felt good. Not frightening. Not then.

You didn't tell her you forgave her. You told her there was nothing to forgive.

Sue tossed and turned again on the sofa. It felt cramped, constraining, uncomfortable. She welcomed the discomfort. It fit how she felt now.

That was about war. That was about a rebellion. This is about torture. How can I forgive that?

And yet her mind flashed back to the shuffling, color-drained humans. Their sluggish movements and their pupilless eyes had made them look empty, unthinking. Like they walked the sands because they had to. Because the same curse that kept the Outcasts here brought them there.

But they'd also raised their hands above their heads and laced them together. Like a ritual.

Like consent.

Could she blame the Outcasts for something these humans had asked for? Could she blame Kara for giving it to them?

And yet, imagining one of those Outcasts with Kara's golden eyes made her heave. She'd been okay with it before. Or so she'd thought. But now…

She closed her eyes and waited for morning, knowing sleep wouldn't come tonight.

CHAPTER TWENTY

Sue slipped out of the apartment and wrapped her clothes around herself. If anyone could see her now, they'd call her frightened. They'd assume she was shaking from nerves, a fragile little beast who couldn't calm herself.

But she was calm now. Still inside. More still than she thought she'd be, fear and joy both gone, somewhere light years away from where she belonged. And Kara wouldn't like what she'd chosen to do.

Kara had good reasons not to like it. It would probably get Sue hurt, or killed. Or at the very least dragged back to Kara in some stranger's claws. She could hear the lecture now: *Your pet is a damned fool, warrior. Take it home and keep it on a shorter leash, for its own protection.*

But something felt right about this, something she could never explain to Kara or to some overbearing Outcast who wanted to protect the silly human. She'd made a choice, even if it was a stupid one. Starfighter pilots did those kinds of things. Maybe not such reckless things. But they made choices and stood by them, even if they seemed risky or impossible.

And Sue would do that now.

She knew the way to the hangar. Her feet remembered it. She was a pilot, and always would be. Even if all she flew was a spacebus.

She slipped down the corridors, not even trying to hide. There would be cameras watching her anyway. And curious Outcasts. She could see one already, turning toward her, orange eyes bright.

"Human. What are you doing here without one of us to escort you?"

Sue puffed out her chest, trying to look so sure of herself the woman wouldn't ask any questions. "I don't need an escort."

"You belong to Kara, don't you?"

Sue winced. "She sent me to check on her craft. We flew it yesterday and some sand got in the, uh—" She tried her best to mimic one of the words she'd heard Kara use for some delicate part.

The woman didn't help. "And you think you could repair it? You aren't one of us. You haven't been here long enough to learn how our ships work."

Shit. "Probably not. But that's the only chance I have of going home."

"Going home?"

"I don't belong here. I'm a living human, not a dead one. And I haven't done the things that make you…" Sue trailed off.

The woman shook her head. "I could help you repair it, if that really is the only problem. But what makes you think you could find your way home? Or are you hoping I'll take you?" She snorted, nostrils flaring. "I don't mind humans, but I'm not flying through a wormhole for one."

Dammit.

"She's not looking for Kara's ship."

Sue turned. She knew that voice.

Dehek swaggered toward them, his wing shadows curling around him. "She's looking for her own ship."

"What are you doing here?" The Outcast woman said it, not Sue. Sue was too shocked to say anything.

"Nothing, Tel."

"I don't believe you."

"I heard Kara's human snuck out, and I couldn't resist seeing it for myself."

He sidled up to them, shadows swishing around him, red streaks bright against his ash-pale skin.

"But it's not just about sneaking out, is it?"

Sue glowered up at Dehek. Glaring at a demon was easier than she thought it would be. "It's none of your business why I came here."

He turned away from her and looked at Tel. "Like I said, she's not looking for Kara's ship."

"Too afraid to say that to my face, Dehek?"

It wasn't courage that made Sue goad him. Or at least, it didn't feel like courage. It felt like anger, and recklessness, and being a stranger in a strange land who was probably never going home. It was something much more bitter, and Sue wasn't sure if she loved it or hated it. But she did wish Dehek would lean in closer so that she could spit in his face.

"Your wreck will kill you if you get into it, human." Tel said it, not Dehek, and Sue felt almost disappointed. "We don't have the materials to repair it, and even if we did it wouldn't last long against the winds."

"That's all right," purred Dehek. "I can take her where she wants to go."

Tel put her hands on her hips. "You're a young fool, not a pilot."

"But I can fly a ship."

"Through a wormhole? You haven't even learned where to find them yet."

Dehek laughed. "Who said anything about a wormhole?"

Sue froze. "This is about me going home."

"Is it?"

"You can't do that, Dehek," Tel said again. "You're no pilot."

"She doesn't want to go home." He sidled closer to Sue. His shadows settled over her and she flinched away. "Do you, little live one?"

"I…" Sue stammered, her throat parched.

"You want to go down there, don't you?"

Words froze in Sue's throat. She wanted to shake her head but couldn't manage it. "Kara took me already," she forced herself to say.

"Kara took you. But that doesn't tell you all you need to know, does it?"

"Kara." She whispered the name.

I chose to protect you.

Sue shook her head. The last thing she wanted right now was Kara in it.

"Kara is this human's owner," Tel said. Sue bit back a curse. *Don't make this harder than it already is. Please.*

Dehek purred. "Yes. And all she wants right now is to take a little trip to the surface. Without Kara."

"That is suicide." Tel's eyes flickered. Sue recognized it as worry.

"No. Just—"

"Absolution," Sue finished for him.

"That is insane!" Tel growled. "You are a living human, and our weapons are designed to be used on the dead."

"I know." Sue bit her lip to keep it from quivering. "But your people could have killed me already, and you didn't. You don't like me much, I know that. But you don't want me dead. You just want me to pay, like the others do."

Dehek smiled.

"And I have things to pay for, just like anyone else."

"So you will let this child take you."

Sue glanced from Dehek to Tel and back again. "If he's willing to take me, yes. If you're willing to take me, I'll go with you instead."

"With me?"

Dehek snickered. "She doesn't like me much. But she knows she needs this."

"She knows you are a fool."

She knows she needs this. Was that true? Or were those the words of a young demon, made seductive by Sue's own despair?

"I want to go," Sue said at last. "I don't want to die, but I want to see for myself."

Dehek grinned, smug.

"Kara told me that no Outcast is born innocent. That every one of you is born without wings, because of what the first ones did."

"Because of our rebellion, yes." Tel's voice was sharp, the beast-burr of her growl still there among the echoes.

"No human is innocent either." *Or at least, I'm not.*

"And you want your own punishment, don't you?" Dehek purred, his voice smooth as an incubus.

"Maybe I do," Sue said, thinking of the boy, thinking of Kara, thinking of herself, ready to hop into a craft with Dehek just to purge herself of it.

I chose to protect you, said a voice in her head again. *And I failed.*

"You feel safe with Dehek?" Tel asked, the light in her eyes flickering again.

"Of course not. I'm a human, not an idiot."

"Well, then."

"But you won't take me, will you?"

"I want no part of this, human. If you want to punish yourself, do it your own way."

"Then I'm going with him."

Chapter Twenty-one

Dehek didn't threaten her.

Dehek didn't do much of anything but keep his eyes on the destination and his claws skating over the controls. He didn't even look at Sue. But he did smirk, the line between his lips a thin thread of red flame.

Sue felt grateful for it. She didn't think she could endure much more of his taunting. She'd get mad, and she didn't want anger. Not right now. Not when she'd decided she deserved his taunting anyway.

There's nothing to forgive. She remembered her own words, the fierce kiss she'd given Kara. She could imagine Kara returning it now.

And yet, she'd asked Kara for the truth and shunned her when she'd found it. Because she couldn't get her memories out of her head. Maybe this would help.

And if it didn't, it would at least mean she'd go back to Kara knowing what she really was. Knowing what parts of her had broken, and what could and couldn't be repaired.

"Descending," Dehek said. Sue looked out the window at a swirl of devouring sand and the rising shape of the obelisk.

He lowered the craft just in front of the obelisk. It hovered in front of the maelstrom.

Sue swallowed hard. Dehek's fingers moved on the console again and the door slid open.

He stepped toward her, shadows swirling. The cracks in his ashen skin blazed with light.

"Human," he said.

Sue slipped off the safety harness and stood. She stepped toward the door, clutching the frame to steady herself.

"Do you want me to jump?"

"Do you want me to drop you?"

"Is that how it works? I guess you should."

There was something in those words, some hint of the anger Sue had felt before. She shot Dehek a look of pure rage.

He laughed in her face. But she heard the nervousness in it, and that was good enough for her.

Clawed hands scooped her up, held her too close to his chest. His scars, his cracks, felt too intimate. She'd gotten close to Kara. She'd seen where Kara broke. But Dehek was a child, and he'd been born shattered.

She wished his shadows would enfold her. But they were stretched out behind him, letting him glide, like the remnants of wings they were.

"All right, human," he said with another rich laugh.

Then he let go, tossing her to the ground below.

❖

The sands battered her cheeks.

She noticed that before anything else, the roughness blasting her skin. She hadn't realized just how fragile her flesh was. It was hot under her feet, too hot, and she wondered too late if she might burst into flame.

It hadn't hurt the damned souls much. As far as Sue could tell, they hadn't even noticed.

But they're not made of the stuff I am. Not anymore. Not skin, not muscle, not bone. They don't know that this tears you apart.

She forced one foot in front of the other. Cruel as Dehek was, he'd at least had the sense or the kindness to drop her near the obelisk.

All she had to do was get to it.

If that. The other humans had just stopped, clasped their hands over their heads, and waited for the Outcasts who would come to punish them.

She stared ahead, wondering. Lightning struck, and she thought she could smell sulfur. Was it raining, or did the sky just do that here?

She could limp her way toward the obelisk and hope it would offer her shelter, hope she could cool her burning feet. But she'd invite torture as soon as she stepped inside it. So should she give up on trying to walk through these wastes, raise her hands now, and hope for a tormentor and a savior in one?

She shuffled a few more steps, her feet scorched. But then the wasteland made the decision for her. A fierce wind battered her, knocking her to her knees on the sands.

She narrowed her eyes, focused her gaze on the obelisk, and lifted her hands above her head.

She didn't wait long. The silver shimmer of a craft appeared above her. She blinked at it. She'd called for a savior, but part of her wondered if it was only a mirage. But under the roar of the winds, she could hear its engine.

A shape emerged from the craft, gray-black and female. Her shadows flared out behind her like the wings they once had been, and gold light blazed from her cracks and scars.

A blast of sand forced Sue to close her eyes.

Gold.

The sands tore at her, ripping through her clothes and into her skin. Why had she come here at all? She didn't know, didn't remember. She only knew it tore at her, exposed her, bared the things that haunted her mind just as it scraped her skin.

Gold. Look.

She forced her eyes open against the grit and sand. *Gold. Gold and gray.*

Kara.

She unclasped her hands and lowered them before she realized why she was doing it. Kara's stony hands curled around hers. They felt warm and smooth and reassuring.

Sue forced her eyes open wider. She looked into a familiar face. Kara's eyes glittered gold, and the scar on her chin glowed bright.

"Kara," she gasped. "You shouldn't have—"

"Shouldn't have followed you? You are a fool, Sue Jones. Are you trying to get yourself killed?"

Sue tried to say something. But the only sound that she could make was a strangled noise.

Kara scooped her up. Firm, solid arms cradled her. They pressed her to a chest warm with vital heat.

Sue wasn't supposed to want it. She wasn't supposed to like it. She was supposed to want punishment and absolution.

But the warmth felt good. Soothing. And she was so tired.

She took a deep breath, cocooned in Kara's embrace, and closed her eyes.

CHAPTER TWENTY-TWO

"So now what?"

The question was too normal. Sue shook her head and forced her eyes open. They stung, dry and scratched. Why did that feel almost ordinary? When had she grown used to this, to questions asked in inhuman voices by glowing people who'd lost their wings?

But it made perfect sense that Kara would ask it, now that Sue had—what? Run off, angry at Kara and angry at herself. Obsessed with the images in her own head, with the way she couldn't make them go away.

But she wasn't in her little room, or even in Kara's apartment.

"The obelisk," she whispered.

Kara nodded.

The walls were red, a deeper and purpler red than the winds outside, like dark blood from a vein. There were small lights embedded in the walls, and the walls gleamed with a strange iridescence, bright crimson against the darker maroon.

Sue shrank back. In the dim light, Kara's scars were a bright blaze. But that only made it harder to see what was here.

"The others?" she gasped out.

"This one is empty. I made sure of it." Kara laughed, a bitter and cold echo. "Whatever you wanted in coming to this place, you don't want to see any more of this. I watched you looking at it. I saw what happened to you after."

"I needed to see it."

"Did you?"

"There are things I can't forgive myself for. Just like those dead ones can't forgive themselves."

The light in Kara's eyes flared. "And all that seeing them did was remind you of it."

Sue stood up and walked away from Kara. How could she explain? Kara had fought and lost and found some way to live with it. Sue saw the boy all the time in her mind.

"You wouldn't understand," Sue said, hating herself for those words. They made her sound like a petulant child.

"Wouldn't I? I see the marks of war on my own body every time I look at my reflection, human." Kara slid her hands down her body.

"And I fought a war, Sue. No one who fights in a war ever forgets. Remember, the people I fought were like me." Kara looked down at herself. "Or I was like them, before our curse."

Sue hung her head. What could she say to that? She'd seen violence, yes, but she'd never seen war. Somehow her dreams and visions, horrible as they were, didn't seem so bad, thinking of that. She'd watched some hooligans beat someone. Maybe even kill him.

But she hadn't tried to kill them first. And she hadn't considered them her kin, either. She shut her lips tightly and watched Kara, saying nothing.

"No one who fights in a war ever forgets it, Sue," Kara said. "And no one who loses forgets what it's like to lose one."

Kara's hands moved again. Sue watched, mesmerized. Kara paused just above one of the cracks that tore through her abdomen. "And then there's what it did to me. These scars."

Sue stepped closer, her skin burning, her leg aching. She wanted to touch Kara, to reach out, to comfort, to soothe. But could she now? She'd run away from Kara and thrown herself at Dehek, of all Outcasts, just to indulge some crazy yen for self-mutilation.

And Kara had come after her. Scooped her up and saved her. And reminded her that whatever she'd endured, Kara had known far worse.

"I'm sorry," she stammered, because it was the only thing she could think of to say. Then she did reach out, pressing her fingertips to one of Kara's arms before she could think better of it.

Kara moved under Sue's hands. Sue froze. Was Kara pulling away?

But Kara didn't move. She stilled under Sue's hands. Sue pressed her fingers against the stony skin until her whole hand, fingertips and fingers and palms, pressed against it. Light flickered in one of the cracks on Kara's arms, and Sue thought she heard Kara sigh.

"My body is broken," Kara said. "My wings are gone. That's mutilation, Sue. Mutilation I see on the bodies of the others every time I look at them. Even the young ones. Even the ones born long after I made my choice. So don't try to tell me that I don't understand."

"This was foolish," Sue answered. "Saying that to your face was worse."

"It was."

"You asked me to forgive you once. I said—"

"That there was nothing to forgive. I remember it."

"If I ask you to forgive me, will you?"

Kara chuckled, low and sad. "I do not know. But I do know what it's like to remember, and not want to."

Sue turned away. There was an alcove in front of her, just wide enough for a human to lean against and wait for…what? Torture? Violence? She shook her head to clear it and looked away, not wanting to know what she was seeing.

"So now what?" she asked, remembering Kara's words to her from before. "Now you take your wayward pet home?"

Kara laughed and licked her lips. "I should. Withdraw what's mine and keep it safe. Under lock and key, if necessary. I said I would protect you. Even if you make that difficult."

Sue shivered. The Outcast woman had said she couldn't go home again. And Kara cared for her and wanted her, both. Even if it was a little bit insulting, why not let herself be kept? She smiled.

But Kara wasn't smiling now. Her lips were closed and set in a grim line. "But if you found a way to wander out here, all by yourself, and let a fool like Dehek fly you into one of the temples, then you must have had a reason."

"It's just like what you said. About the war. About remembering. I close my eyes and I see the boy. I can't stop thinking about him. And once I heard about you, about what the Outcasts do…I don't know. It haunted me."

Kara nodded. "That is how it is for many of the dead. Though they've done far worse than you. You fear your inaction cost another human his life. These people killed, violated, maimed. They chose it. And kept choosing it."

"Until they died."

"Only when they came here did they see what they deserved."

Deserved. Did they deserve it? She'd thought she deserved it, when Dehek dumped her out here. Then Kara had rescued her.

"You are different, Sue," Kara said, her voice soft. Her clawed hands curled. "You don't see it, but you are."

"Maybe. But I can't make myself believe it."

"Then you need someone to show it to you."

Chapter Twenty-three

"That is what these temples are for," Kara said.

"For punishment?" Sue stepped toward the alcove. An X-shaped cross hung in the shadow there, chains and bonds hanging from it.

"For absolution."

"What's the difference?" But even as Sue asked it, she slipped out of the clothes she'd brought with her. It seemed only right, somehow, to stand naked in this room. To slip out of garments that the sand had scratched and torn and stained red, and expose herself, as she was.

To Kara, and to whatever holiness might exist here. Sue had called it an obelisk, in her mind, but Kara had called it a temple.

"Punishment is about doing wrong and paying the price for it," Kara said. "Sometimes, a price chosen by the ones who feel that you wronged them. Not by you yourself. It lets those who hate or fear you feel vindicated or avenged."

"And absolution?"

"Absolution is about letting go."

Sue leaned against the cross. Her breasts pressed against it. It was warm. Had the Enemy made this? His torture house for the people he'd rejected? Or had the Outcasts built this place, like they'd built the Rings?

"The boy," Sue whispered. "The things in my head. The dreams. The blood. You."

Kara stepped closer behind her. The shadow of Kara's wings fell over her, heavy with a warmth of its own.

Kara picked up the chains and wrapped one of the cuffs around Sue's wrists but didn't fasten it. "I can't promise you those things will ever leave you, Sue. They don't leave the dead ones." Her eyes flickered. "They haven't left me."

"You were in a war, though."

Kara sighed. "I was. And war is unlike anything else. But I shouldn't have said what I did to you."

"No, you're right. What I saw, what I did, what I didn't do… there will always be something worse in the world. Always be someone who's known worse. I'll never know what you know." She twitched her shoulders. "I never had any wings to lose."

Kara reached out her other hand and ran it down Sue's back. Sue shivered.

"I am glad of that, Sue Jones," Kara said. "We Outcasts were born a prideful race. That is both a good thing and a bad one." She slid a single claw tip over the ridge of Sue's spine, careful not to dig or cut. Sue froze under it, her skin tingling.

"So this won't make me forget," Sue said. It wasn't a question.

"Nothing will make you forget. But it might help you to remember less, if you let it."

"Then I guess I've got to do it."

Kara's hand splayed out against the flesh of Sue's back. "Not necessarily. Not unless you feel that this is what you need. There are many ways to let go, Sue Jones. If you'd like to find another one, I can take you home, and we can find another one together."

Sue shook her head. "No. I wanted to see this. I wanted to know what your people do. What happens to the human men and women who go to hell."

"All right." Kara clasped the cuff around Sue's wrist. "But I can't do to you what we do to the dead."

Sue's head snapped to the side. She stared at Kara. "We? What *we* do to the dead? Not what *you* do to them?"

"I will do this for you, Sue, because you asked for it, and because I know why. But I will never do it to the damned again." For a long moment, Kara let her hand linger in the center of Sue's back. Then she moved it away, lifted Sue's arm, and clasped the second cuff around it.

Sue turned her head again, facing the wall. She took another deep breath and studied the iridescent streaks in the wall, imagined meaning in the patterns of the light. She was making things up, of course. But doing it soothed her. Helped her forget what would come next.

"In my dream," Sue said, "the Outcast carried a scourge. It had lots of tails, and all of them were tipped with fire."

Kara's voice reached her from somewhere far away. "Fire wouldn't harm a ghost. A soul isn't made of flesh and blood. But it would harm you."

"Then what do you use?"

"Don't worry." Sue could hear Kara's grin. "I'll find something."

Hearing her felt almost good too, a little shock of expectation, half eagerness and half fear. Sue pressed her legs together and let herself savor it as best she could.

She heard Kara rummaging through something and closed her eyes to force herself not to turn around and look. Then she heard Kara's footsteps, getting louder and closer. She tensed, expecting a blow.

But instead, she only felt Kara's hand on her again, pressed to her back.

"What are you doing?" she stammered, as Kara's hand slipped down to her waist and over her buttocks. "You're supposed to be hurting me, not—"

But Kara only slid her hand over the curve of Sue's buttock and slipped her fingers over Sue's pelvis.

"I am going to whip you," Kara said. "I said that I would and I will." She moved her fingers again, let them slip over Sue's mound. Sue gave a strangled little sound and canted her hips, pushing her ass out to let Kara touch it.

She hadn't come here for that, no. She'd come here for something very different. But she was tired, and Kara had saved her. And Kara was a demon warrior in her prime. If she said this was going to hurt eventually, well, then it was going to hurt.

If Kara wanted her first, why not let her do this? Sue spread her legs wider.

Kara slid her fingers over Sue's labia, wetting them with Sue's moisture. She slipped one finger lower, finding Sue's clit and moving on it. Sue closed her eyes and bucked her hips. *I'm not sure if this is supposed to redeem me, but I sure as hell don't mind.*

Kara slipped her fingers in. Sue moved with her, finding the rhythm.

Then Kara pulled away. She slid her fingers out of Sue and traced them over her thigh.

"Why did you stop?" Sue gasped, her heart pounding.

"The question is why I started in the first place," Kara said, still tracing a claw over the sensitive skin of Sue's inner thigh. "And the answer is: because this is a ritual. Even if it's a ritual of hell, fit for the corrupted dead and not for the living. This isn't just about your shame and guilt, Sue Jones. This is about letting go."

She slid her hand up Sue's side, the claws an almost tickling tease.

"That doesn't mean it's about pleasure." Kara spread out her hands across Sue's back. She tilted her claws inward, not pricking Sue's skin, but offering a promise of danger. "But there is no sin in taking pleasure in it. Not if that helps you to forgive yourself."

Kara bent down and pressed her lips to Sue's shoulder. Then she opened her mouth and pressed the tips of her fangs to Sue's skin.

"Go ahead," Sue breathed. "Bite. You've done it before, and I liked it."

Kara drew away. "I want to. But for this ritual, I need you pristine."

Sue turned to look at her. She wasn't sure she'd wanted to see what Kara held in her hands. But something compelled her to turn and look, all the same.

The whip Kara held had thin strands of what looked like leather. Sue had never been whipped before, but she guessed that it would sting, and her muscles tensed in expectation.

It also wasn't on fire. But Sue could see small streaks of light curl over it. She looked over at Kara. Was Kara humming? Sue thought of the magic the musicians made through their song. Or was there some kind of energy moving over the tails of the whip?

Whatever it was, it wasn't as intense as what she'd seen. Much less than what she'd dreamed.

I'm with Kara. Kara will take care of me.

Sue turned back toward the wall again. She heard the whip move behind her and felt a small breeze of air as Kara practiced a few swings.

It fell lightly against her shoulders, barely a blow. Probably Kara testing her aim. Or being kind. Still, it did sting. And after the fire of the blow, an electric crackle, like lightning crawling over the places it had been.

That wasn't a blow. Not really. But—

I can do this. I can endure this.

Sue closed her eyes and let her images come. Let herself imagine it. Red liquid on asphalt and closed eyes and brown skin. Buttons pinned to a jacket, flashing political slogans, over and over, heedless of what had happened to their owner.

She heard the whirl of Kara's whip through the air.

Then it crashed against her skin.

It stung, a bright fierce pain that sped through all her nerves, shocking every part of her awake. Sue opened her mouth and gulped in air.

She also opened her eyes. The image shattered, ripped away from her by the fierce sting.

But that was nowhere near as hard as an Outcast warrior could hit, and Sue knew it. *I'm with Kara, and Kara will protect me.*

Kara swung the whip with a slow and steady rhythm. It burned, scorching lines of fire into her skin. And the electric crackle that came with it made sure that the burn lingered.

And yet the rhythm came with its own strange reassurance. *In another moment, it will burn me.*

Sue focused on her images. The boy. The dream. Kara's face, transformed and transfigured into something forbidding and alien and angry.

Each one, the blows tore through, the tails of the whip rending and tearing at the image and drawing her back.

Here.

Into the temple, with its red walls.

Into her burning skin.

She swayed with the rhythm of the whip, expecting the blows, twisting into them. Opening her mouth and shrieking, half because it did hurt and half to give vent to the sounds she'd never let herself make then.

It burned. But it meant she was alive.

And it meant she was with Kara, and Kara was with her.

The sensation built within her skin, a fire like the living fire in Kara. It tore through the numbness, ripped Sue from the dreams that froze her, and brought her home to herself at last. She tilted her hips and heard herself moan.

Kara swung the whip across Sue's buttocks. It tore lines of flame over them, just like Kara's claws might, and Sue screamed out a welcome. All around her, the shadows of her past crouched, waiting to take her over. With every blow, they receded, the shocks of sensation awakening her nerves and driving them all away.

The whip crashed over her again and again. Sue lost count of how many times. She moved to Kara's rhythm again, tilting her hips, presenting each buttock to the whip and its electric aftermath.

At long last, Kara lowered her arm.

Sue's hair—the hair Kara had cut—clung to her forehead, plastered there by sweat. Her throat ached from screaming and moaning, and some of the moisture on her face was probably not sweat but tears.

Kara stepped over to her, reached out to touch her buttocks, her back. It reawakened a fresh sting, but Sue didn't mind that at all. *Yes. Touch me. Be with me.*

Here.

What Sue said when she found the strength to speak again was more vulgar than that, but no less heartfelt.

CHAPTER TWENTY-FOUR

"You want me to do what?" Kara asked, the echoing voice rich with mischief.

"You heard me." Sue smiled. "Fuck me."

Kara chuckled and ran her hands over Sue's welts, sending new sparks of sensation through her tender skin.

Sue laughed right back at her. "You're a demon, according to us humans. Don't tell me you've never heard those words before."

"Very well then. I won't."

Kara slapped at Sue's thighs. It might have startled her before, but under the bright burn of the flogging, it just felt like a firm touch, with all of Kara's warrior strength behind it. Sue spread her legs wider.

Kara didn't hesitate. She sank two fingers into Sue with a confident thrust.

Sue moaned and arched back against Kara, savoring the feeling of being filled. Kara's whip had seared her, pushed her, ripped away her illusions. This, at the end of it, was just sex: rough and welcome.

"Harder," Sue begged. Kara growled and obliged, driving deep. The friction and rhythm flooded Sue with sensation. The bright burn of the welts on her back and buttocks only fed its tide. The bright burn of being alive, asked for and embraced.

Sue threw back her head. Kara was heat and light under stone skin. Sue was only human, but every part of her blazed now, overflowing with life and light. Kara slipped another finger in and Sue hissed and shivered as it stretched her open wider.

Sue moved back on Kara's fingers, heedless of anything but her own hunger. *Yes. This. More.*

With a slow, deliberate motion, Kara pulled her fingers almost out of Sue, leaving only her fingertips inside. Sue whimpered at the loss. Then Kara slammed her fingers in again.

Sue froze, her body locking hard around Kara's fingers. She cried out again as the spasm overtook her, a wordless affirmation.

❖

"Are your visions gone?"

Sue blinked, her sex twitching with aftershocks. She opened her eyes to see Kara's face inches from her own, her lips curled in a smile.

Sue shook her head to clear it. "I…I don't know. I won't know for sure until I sleep and don't dream about him." She gave a wry laugh. "For several nights in a row, probably."

She winced at that. But Kara only nodded. "The memories never leave us. Not for good."

Yeah. You said that before. The difficult ones are the ones that don't leave us. And you were right. "But they're not in my head right now, and that's a start."

All you've left room for in my head right now is you.

Thanks.

Kara slipped the restraints off Sue's wrists, one after the other. She massaged the places where the cuffs had been. That made Sue wince a little, sensation and discomfort returning all at once. But all things considered, she'd rather have Kara touching her than not.

Her arms free now, she wrapped them around Kara's back, seeking out the scarred places and pressing her fingertips to them.

"Sue," Kara growled. "This isn't about me. This is about you."

Sue clutched Kara tighter. "No. This isn't just about me. This is about us. You made it about us when you came after me." She moved her hands over the scars.

Kara made another rumbling little sound, but to Sue's immense satisfaction this one sounded a little bit more like a purr.

"I thought it was about me," Sue went on, sliding her hands down Kara's back. "I wanted it to be about me and nothing else. Then you came after me."

Kara snorted. "That is true."

Sue grinned. "So you see? This one's on you. You're just going to have to live with that."

Kara chuckled. "Very well." She wrapped her arms around Sue and Sue sank into them. "But you don't know how tired you are. You snuck out in the middle of the night—you couldn't have slept—and found your way to the hangar. Then you convinced Dehek, of all Outcasts, to fly you to the surface."

"Yeah." Sue let Kara hold her up. It felt good to sink into her arms like this, her skin still stinging from the beating, her cunt still pulsing with the last of her aftershocks.

Kara lifted Sue effortlessly and cradled her in her arms. Sue snickered. *Is that because you want to hold me, or is that because you're not sure where to put me down?* But that, too, felt good, the welts on her back pressed against Kara's stony skin and the warmth of the cracks in it. She wriggled to show Kara she liked it.

Kara grinned. "And that isn't all of it," she said, as if Sue hadn't interrupted. "Then you crawled halfway here in a sandstorm. Something even the dead don't like to endure. And offered yourself to the ritual of absolution afterward."

"And to your hands."

"Yes. And to my hands. But my point is, Sue Jones, you must be exhausted."

Sue let her eyes close. "Yes. I am. I could fall asleep right here in your arms."

"Without visions of the boy?" Sue couldn't see Kara smiling, but she could hear it in her tone.

"Without visions of the boy," Sue agreed. "But are you really saying that you want me to fall asleep right here in the middle of your, uh, temple?"

"Let me take you back to our craft first."

Our craft. Not "my craft." Ours.

"I'd like that," Sue said.

Kara carried her to the door. "You won't like the storm outside. Though it seems to have died down a little. You really must have wanted to punish yourself before. I'm surprised you got as far as you did."

Sue winced, bracing herself for the sands. "No, I won't like the storm outside." She opened her eyes, made sure to look up into Kara's face. "But I'll like you taking me there. You have to glide to get to the ship."

Kara's eyes widened. "I—"

"You can't fly any more, no. But you can glide and you can hover. Storm or no storm, sand or no sand, I want to be in your arms when you do, Kara of the Outcasts."

CHAPTER TWENTY-FIVE

As soon as they got back to Kara's apartment, Kara laid her down.

Sue could tell Kara was tired. Gliding wasn't flying, and sandstorms weren't friendly to beings whose skin was filled with cracks. Kara's wing shadows hovered behind her, their shifting sluggish.

But she'd perked up as soon as Sue lay down.

The protector thing again, probably. Sue closed her eyes, remembering Kara holding her tightly, the winds carrying them, the growl in Kara's throat as she battled the weather.

Kara wouldn't let Sue lie on her back. She walked over to the cooling cupboard and drew out a small bottle of ointment. She spread the ointment on her fingers and then pressed it to Sue's welts.

Sue hissed as it made contact. Her welts were fresh and still stung. But the ointment was cool and the burn in her flesh quieted. It didn't hurt, not really, not unless Kara was touching the welts. Sue found she welcomed that, a reminder of what had passed between them.

Kara seemed to like touching them, too. She ran her fingers over Sue's back and buttocks even after she'd dabbed the ointment on them, sometimes careful to avoid the welts, sometimes touching them.

"It is a ritual," she said, "and I performed it for your sake. But I like seeing my marks on you, my little human."

Sue leaned her head on her elbows and turned to look at Kara. "Little human. I'm not so sure I like that."

Kara paused. "You are not like us. You're—"

"Just a mortal. I know."

"That isn't what I meant."

"Yeah, you did. I remember what you showed me when you sang." Sue closed her eyes and pictured it: the dark-skinned woman, her glowing skin, her wings, so bright a white Sue hadn't quite been able to make them out. The inner fire in her eyes and mouth, the hints of what became her horns once she fell.

Kara's hands on Sue's back stilled. "When I sang?" She hung her head, the great horns pointing down. "That was me before the war. Before I lost my wings."

"I know."

"I haven't been that for a long time."

Sue looked directly at Kara. "That's exactly what I meant. Neither one of us is perfect, Kara. Me or you."

Kara sighed and looked down at herself. She moved one of her hands from Kara's back and traced the contours of one of the cracks in her skin. "That is so."

"That's why I left."

"Which you should never have done," Kara whispered. She squirted more of the gel onto her fingertips and ran them over Sue's welts again. The gel's chill soothed the welts' sting. "There is no point to feeling shame over that."

Sue let herself savor the feeling of the gel on her welts. She closed her eyes and took a deep breath. "No, there isn't. But I ran off for a reason. From this, from my dreams."

"From me."

"No. From what I'd learned. From you telling me that this really was hell, that the people on the surface are human." Sue shivered, remembering.

Kara said nothing. She ran her hands over Sue's back again. Sue sighed into it, trying to let herself relax. Trying to remember the pleasure she'd just felt under Kara's hands. Trying to forget the serious conversation and just let go.

"That the Enemy ordered us to torture humans." Kara looked down, her expression unreadable.

"Yeah. And that you did it willingly."

"Even though you wanted to see it." Kara snarled, showing her fangs. "Even though you asked me to bring you down to the surface and show you."

Sue closed her eyes. "I thought I needed to know." She reached up to grab Kara's hand. She laced her small, brown fingers, with Kara's clawed and gray ones.

"I should never have agreed to bring you to the surface," Kara said. But she tightened her grip on Sue's hand, clutching hard.

"I had to see it eventually," Sue said. "But you were right. I wasn't ready. I wasn't ready and I ran."

"And now?"

Sue gestured around the room. "Look around you. Look at this stuff, this place. These Rings."

Kara did look around but said nothing.

"You Outcasts built a whole world for yourselves," Sue went on. "You were supposed to live on the surface, to work and toil and suffer like your human victims. Am I right?"

"You are."

"And instead, you Outcasts—you glorious, rebellious bastards, fighting even after you lost—decided fuck it, hell no, we're not living in a wasteland. We're building ships and cities and living like we want to, banishment or no banishment." She looked up at Kara. "What about that one? Am I right about that too?"

Kara turned back to look at her and smiled.

Sue didn't say anything. She just waited.

"But what does this have to do with our duties in the temples?"

"You're rebels. You live the way you want. You always have and always will. Enemy or no Enemy, scars or no scars."

Kara's cracks flashed with light. "Yes."

"Then if you give the ritual of absolution to the dead humans, if you torture the damned, you do it because you chose to."

Kara shook her head and snarled. "I already told you I didn't want to do it. That I'd given it up. That if it had been any other human down there, any soul but yours, I would never have gone down to the surface again."

"Then you don't like this ritual?"

Kara looked down at her. "I liked it with you." She unwound her hand from Sue's and traced one of the welts on Sue's back with the tip of a claw. Sue froze, not wanting a stray movement to cut her.

"I liked it too. But that's because you were helping me. The others—"

"They are damned. Beyond redemption."

"So they just"—Sue shuddered in spite of herself, and Kara pulled her hand away—"deserve it, over and over? I didn't."

"They think they do." Kara growled. "They are damned, as you say. Or so the Enemy tells them, and so they believe." She shook her head. "I want no part of it any longer."

Sue lifted herself up on her hands. "Not even with me?"

Kara's frown became a smile, fanged and bright. "You're different. You wanted redemption."

"Redemption. Isn't that the Enemy's business? Savior and redeemer," Sue recited, a faraway title from a story she suddenly wished she'd paid more attention to.

"We are rebels, Sue Jones. We live as we want to, like you said."

"Which means?"

"Which means if my rituals can offer you redemption I will give it to you. I like what you are, Sue Jones."

Sue grinned.

"That is why I call you my human."

"It was the 'little' part I objected to. Not so much the 'my.'"

Chapter Twenty-six

Kara's eyes widened. "You want to be mine?"

"You were right from the beginning. I already am yours." She shimmied under Kara's hands again. Kara purred.

But this wasn't just about fun. "Doesn't really matter if I wanted to be or not," Sue finished.

Kara pulled away. "Sue."

"I'm human and you're not. To the other Outcasts who don't know me, that makes me your pet. Just like you said." *But don't you run from me, Ms. Warrior.* "Don't worry. I'm not angry. As long as I'm here, it is what it is."

"As long as you're here."

"Yep. Which is probably going to be a hell of a long time."

"Is that so?" Kara narrowed her eyes. "The others told me you went to the hangar looking for your own ship, not for mine."

Sue sucked in a breath. What could she say to that? "I did. At first."

Kara sighed. "This place. I know it's not your home."

"My home is pretty awful. Riots, rickety buses that barely fly. Potholes if you aren't flying."

She let out a little laugh, harsher than she'd meant for it to be. This place, these Rings, were so pristine, floating above their little hellstorm. Even here in Kara's apartment, everything looked too clean. Too perfect. Sue found herself wanting some cracked concrete, rusted metal, walls thick with graffiti proclaiming *Bob was here* or *I'd rather be on Cyprus IV* or *Fuck the government* or *Don't worry! They're always watching you.*

Life in the colonies was frightening. Unstable. Uneasy. You had to take care of yourself. Immortal warriors didn't just descend from the sky to make sure you would be okay. But the life you lived there was yours, and no one else's.

And then there were the people. Everyone here was an Outcast. Everyone here had horns and stony skin, and blazing scars that testified to the wings they'd once flown on. No one looked like Sue or sounded like her.

She hadn't bothered to miss the other colonists. She hadn't had time to think of them. She'd done so much. Flown through the wormhole. Made it here. Met beings she'd thought were aliens. Explored their world.

Then she'd discovered what the Outcasts really were. And then she'd journeyed to the surface, seen the dead ones, gone into the temple and submitted to the whip.

So little time in any of that to just miss people. She found herself thinking of that old boyfriend, the one with such a gentle touch. She hadn't seen him in years. What was he doing now? Where was he? The same colony they'd both lived in back then? Or had he run off, looking for a better place?

Had he found one?

And what about her other friends? Or even the people who rode her spacebus every morning and every night? Had they noticed she was gone? Did they miss her?

"You're quiet for someone who doesn't miss your home," Kara said. She turned away and looked out the window.

Sue slid up on one elbow and watched Kara stare out at the storm. "It was a pretty bad place. You Outcasts have a nice place here, all things considered. The Rings are clean. The ships aren't always breaking down." She grinned. "The food's good." *Even if I am beginning to really miss solid food.*

"But it is not our home," Kara said.

Oh. Right. That.

"I'm sorry," Sue began. "I didn't mean it like that."

Kara turned to face her and shook her head. "There is nothing to apologize for. We have not seen our true home in eons. The young ones like your friend Dehek were born here. The Rings are the only place many of us know."

"Then why did you ask about me?"

"Because you still have a home, Sue. It may be far away, there may be a wormhole between you and it, but…" Kara looked out toward the window again. "It's still your home. If you found your way back, the people there would welcome you."

Sue shook her head, chuckling. "Some of them might. But I told you about the riots. That thing with the boy isn't the only violence I've seen. It's just the only time I thought I might have been able to do something about it. And I couldn't."

"And this place?"

"This place is peaceful. Yeah, sure, Dehek hates me. And if he has his way other Outcasts probably will too. But the older ones know you and respect you. And because of that they respect me."

"It's not just because of that."

"Are you saying they like me? 'Hey, everyone, look at Kara's human pet'?"

Kara chuckled. "For some of them, perhaps. But that isn't what I meant. Our war happened an age ago, and our memories are long. We've lived here a long time. And as you said, we started out doing what we thought the Enemy wanted of us. Living on the surface, tormenting the human dead as our own exile tormented us. But then, over the many millennia, we changed."

"You built the Rings."

"We built the Rings. We made homes for ourselves. We found food that we enjoyed and we cultivated it. When we moved to the Rings, it didn't end our suffering. But we began to believe that our suffering, perhaps, was no longer required."

Sue smiled. "Good. But what's that got to do with humans? With me?"

"We were brought here to suffer. To make the unforgiven humans suffer, as we did. If our suffering was no longer required, why should we require yours?"

"So things are better here. You've grown."

"We have. But this place is still not our home, and we still know it." Kara reached out a hand toward the window, her claws grasping at something long gone. "There were meadows, and oceans, and valleys. And boundless skies, where we flew. The winds made music, and our voices echoed it."

"I'm sorry. I can't even imagine what it must be like to be here after being…" She trailed off. *In heaven,* if you believed what the old religion said. But if hell was a planet, did that mean heaven was small, too?

She couldn't say so. Not to Kara. Not right now.

Kara shook her head. "I was supposed to guide them. To lead them in war, yes, but also—"

"To protect them," Sue finished for her.

Kara didn't look back at her. But the shadows around her floated and settled, soft as a sigh. "You're an exile too. Like us."

"It's not a big deal," Sue tried. But it was. Of course it was.

"You were looking for your own ship before Dehek distracted you."

"I was, in the beginning. Yeah."

"You miss your home as well."

Sue thought of the old boyfriend, his careful fingers. She thought of the first woman she'd kissed, a girl with pale skin and blue eyes that wrinkled up when she smiled and dirty blond hair that always hung down in her face. Sue hadn't loved her, but she'd liked her, liked what they'd done, liked what she'd found out about herself and how it made her feel.

And it made her think of other things, little things. The scuffed toes of her old girlfriend's boots. Here, wearing clothes was a weird thing. A thing Sue did, and no one else. No one except the dead.

And here there were no other humans. Except the dead.

"I hadn't thought about it. But yeah, I guess I do."

Chapter Twenty-seven

Sue grabbed at Kara's hand. She reached up to her own face, making Kara cup her fingers around Sue's chin. "What is this really about?"

"This place is not your home," Kara said again. She ran a claw over Sue's lips. "It can never offer you what your home offers."

Sue wrapped her other hand around Kara's head. She slid her hand over one of Kara's horns. Its surface, grooved and then pointed, felt strange, alien, unlike anything else she'd touched before. She'd seen pictures and holograms of animals with horns, but out in the colonies, you'd never get to touch anything like that.

Which was exactly why she touched Kara's horn now. Kara's eyes flickered, and her mouth opened, exposing a little hint of gold.

That must mean you like it.

Yes. Yes. This. Show yourself to me.

"Is that what you're scared of?" Sue whispered.

Kara's eyes locked on Sue's, a blaze of gold. But then she looked down. "It's not about wanting, Sue. Home always finds you in the end. Even when you're sure you've let it go, it stays with you." She closed the distance between them, pressing her lips to Sue's. Sue slid her hand from Kara's horn and wrapped it around the back of Kara's head. She opened her mouth wide and let Kara swallow her moan.

Kara's hands wrapped around her back. Little bursts of sensation flared through the welts where Kara touched them.

Sue slid her own hands over Kara's back and shoulders. But she knew what she was really looking for. She traced the edges of the scars.

Kara hissed, and when Sue finally broke the kiss, she showed her fangs. But she wasn't resisting, not this time. Sue made soft, encouraging sounds and traced the scars with her fingers, over and over.

This is what you endured and what you lost. And I want all of it, Kara of the Outcasts.

Sue curled her fingers inward. It wouldn't sting, not like the whip had. But it might burn, just a little, and that might make Kara remember, just like the whip had made Sue.

Kara sucked in another breath and hissed again. Sue watched her carefully. But she tilted her head and opened her mouth and let out a shaky breath that sounded a little like a moan, so Sue curled her fingers tighter.

She moved down to kiss Kara's neck, to press her head into her shoulder and nuzzle and lick. Kara hummed, a steady note almost like her song. There wasn't quite a vision in it, not without harmony and words, but Sue could see something anyway: light in darkness, swirling like a distant galaxy.

She kissed her way down to Kara's breasts, her lips feeling the warrior firmness of Kara's body. Her lips curled around the hard bud of Kara's nipple and sucked. Her hips rocked in sympathy and a little scintilla of pleasure made her sex spasm along with it.

Kara's hands tightened around her head, and her claws twined in Sue's hair. Hair that Kara had not just cut, but had trimmed with those very claws. Had made hers, the jagged lines of the warrior, an echo of her scars.

Yes. Yes.

"Lie down," she said to Kara.

Kara purred and followed Sue's hands, settling down on the bed.

Sue leaned down to kiss her way down Kara's chest, pausing at one of the cracks. She kissed it, feeling the warmth against her lips, and then licked along its edge. Kara purred and pressed Sue's head down, closer. Sue smiled against Kara's skin.

She traced her way down to Kara's stomach, still kissing and licking, and ran her hands over Kara's sides. She splayed out her fingers, wanting to create as much sensation as she could. Kara made another contented sound and canted her hips.

Yes. Yes. Sue's mouth watered. She remembered the thick ambrosia of Kara's wetness staining her fingers and ached to taste it. She moved faster, sliding her head down toward Kara's hips, finding another scar and tracing her tongue along its edges.

Kara parted her legs, and Sue traced her way over the hairless mound, smooth as a sculpture. But Kara was warm under her lips and tongue, and shifted under her to admit her better.

Sue opened her mouth to taste Kara's wetness. It was thick, like honey, and it tasted crisp. Like clear water Sue had drank once, bottled on some faraway and unpolluted planet. And under it all, a faint hint of other tastes. A whiff of spice and sharpness.

She couldn't place them all. *I'm just a mere mortal, after all.* But Kara's hand wrapped around her head and pressed her closer, and she lost herself in it.

She lapped at Kara's clit. Kara pushed back against her, grinding against her lips and tongue with possessive abandon. She gasped, took a deep breath, and moved faster, Kara's clit a hard pebble against her tongue.

She gripped at Kara's hips, pulling her closer. Kara's hand tightened in her hair, the tips of her claws a prick against Sue's scalp. Then Kara roared out a cry of pleasure, her clit pressed to Sue's lips and tongue as her body shuddered.

Sue clutched Kara's hips. *Yes. Yes. Show me. Show me all of yourself. Show me everything.*

CHAPTER TWENTY-EIGHT

"There is someone I want you to meet," Kara said.

Sue stretched. She would have reached for her clothes, given that Kara was talking about going out. But being naked now, with Kara, in a place where clothes didn't really matter, felt surprisingly good. "Someone?"

"I don't know if you mean to stay or leave. But if you do mean to stay, if you want to know us, you need to see us for who we really are."

"You want me to meet more of you?"

"I want you to meet one. I want you to meet the one who led our rebellion, and who rules our world."

Sue froze. "The Enemy," she choked out.

Kara's eyes widened and brightened. "Our leader, yes."

Sue bit her lip. Why had she called him that? The Outcasts used that name for Sue's forgotten god, not for their leader. And whatever she should call him, Kara had followed him. Into a war that had cost her everything. Her wings. Her beauty. Her rank. Her home.

"I'm sorry," Sue said. "I don't know why I said that."

"Because you've been taught all your life to fear him. To fear us."

Sue looked down. "Yeah, I guess that's true."

"That's why I want to bring you to him. Because if you stay, you need to know what we believe. What we stand for and who we choose to serve."

"You still serve him?"

Kara nodded. "He has ruled us from the beginning. We are not what we once were. We were soldiers. Rebels. Fighters who needed a commander. Now we're—"

"People," Sue finished for her.

Kara tilted her head. "People?"

Sue waved vaguely. "This place. It isn't for soldiers. I mean, you were a soldier. A warrior. But people like Dehek weren't even born when the revolution happened. The Rings are a city. A whole bunch of cities connected to each other. Not a barracks or a citadel."

Kara nodded. "That is so."

"And your leader? Your lord? Whatever I'm supposed to call him?"

"We called him the Bringer of Light."

Sue chuckled at that. "And did he?"

Kara bristled. "Are you looking for me to defy him?"

"No! I just mean that your rebellion failed. You're not soldiers any more. Why would you want me to see him?"

"Because you aren't one of us."

Anger flared through Sue. "You're not starting this again. Not after all we've been through. Not after how far we've come together."

"I am not starting anything, you damn fool human. I am only saying this: You are torn between what you have found here and your memories of your home. Is that not true?"

"Kara, I already told you. I don't even know if there's a way for me to go home any more. I was just running away. I want you. I want this. You don't need to worry about something that can't happen."

"That can't happen or that won't? You are an exile, at least for the moment. Just like me. This place is not your home, and you know it. You've found comfort here, found hope here…but this is not your home."

"So?"

"So choosing to stay is about more than simply settling down."

"Not if there's no chance of going home anyway!"

Kara growled. Her claws curled, slashing at the air in front of Sue. Sue froze. *I know Kara. Kara cares for me. I'm safe with Kara.*

"Don't speak to me of having no chances, human," Kara said, her voice cold. "I have no chance. The Outcasts have no chance. We were banished. You were not."

Damn it. "I didn't mean it like that."

"All it takes for you to find your way back is to find someone who knows enough about wormholes to help you do it."

"Kara, I already told you, I've got no plans to do it."

"Not now. But if you mean to stay here, you need to choose this place as your home." The shadows around Kara fluttered. "And to do that, you need to know this place. And the people who made it what it is. Including the one who led our rebellion and who leads us now."

"And you want what? For me to swear allegiance to him? To a guy my people's religion tells me is the ultimate evil?"

Kara shook her head. "I don't want you to swear allegiance to anything, Sue. Not to him. Not even to me."

"I thought I was your pet."

"That's different."

"Good. I'm glad it is. But what are you looking for? What is it you really want from me?"

Kara sighed. "You could belong here if you wanted to. You could be mine, mine for real." She chuckled, grasping at air with her clawed hands. "I would like that."

I'm sure you would. I might, too.

Or is that the problem? That I might?

"Or you could…stay," Kara went on. "Remain, but be a stranger. Sometimes that is all someone can do. But whether you decide that you belong, or that you don't but you choose to stay anyway, you must know what you are doing. Who the people are that you claim, whether you call them kin or comrades."

Sue took a deep breath. "And you think to really do that I need to meet the one I still keep calling the Enemy."

"You need to know us. You need to see us for all that we are. You've seen our Rings. You've heard our songs. You've seen our bodies and our scars. But you need to know how we got those scars, and why we take pride in them, even though they're supposed to be a marker of our shame. And to know that, you need to know what we were fighting for. And who we were fighting for."

Sue sighed. "All right. I'll do it." *But you're wrong. All I need to know is you.*

CHAPTER TWENTY-NINE

Sue wrapped herself up in her clothes. Wearing them had become almost silly now, but she liked the thought of having something between herself and the Lord of the Outcasts. Protector, Kara might be, but could she protect Sue from her own leader? Sue clutched the jacket around her chest, even though the hallway was warm.

The Rings grew bigger as they moved through them, the lights brighter. They blared from the ceiling and the walls, shining against Kara's gray skin.

Sue walked behind her, like she'd done before. Outcasts whispered as she passed, and she lowered her head, trying to look the part of Kara's pet. But she'd learned enough of the Outcasts' language to catch words in their whispers.

Most seemed to find it funny. Some odd quirk of Kara's, like Sue had said a while ago. Collecting strays. She could hear it in their voices, calling her a possession. Calling Kara a collector. Some said it with amusement, others with derision. But so far, no one did more than stare.

In fact, the people here seemed too poised to do more. They walked with careful, prideful posture, their backs straight, their horns arching toward the skies.

Sue looked around for Dehek and his crowd, but they were nowhere to be found. *Thank heaven for small mercies. Or hell. Whichever.*

But it was more than that, she realized. None of these Outcasts looked like Dehek. None of them were young.

She looked over the broad body of a slate-pale Outcast. His horns were massive, far larger than Kara's, curling up and up and up. His cracks, pale yellow, tore through his chest and back in dozens of places.

Are those all scars? Sue looked from him to Kara and back again. How old were the Outcasts who had fought in their great war? He looked as old as Kara.

Sue watched the way he looked at Kara. An incline of his head, a low sound like the beginning of an Outcast song. *That's respect. It has to be.*

And Kara nodded back to him, lowering her eyes.

Sue slipped closer to Kara. "These are all warriors," she whispered, hoping her voice was low enough for them not to overhear.

"Yes," Kara answered.

"Your comrades."

"Yes."

Sue watched a few more of them pass by. One fixed her gaze on Sue, and Sue lowered her head again, hoping it looked deferential enough. The woman sniffed the air and snorted, nostrils a bright angry red, but she passed by Kara without comment.

"This is where the warriors live," Sue said.

"Most of us, yes."

"But not you."

"No."

Kara didn't say more. Sue caught someone else staring and went quiet.

The light was blazing bright here, the ceiling high and wide. Hollow beams wove in and out, the lights embedded between them, glaring down on Sue and Kara. The lights from the hallway were almost as bright.

What was it Kara had called her leader? Bringer of Light?

They stopped in front of a pair of closed metal doors, so polished they could have been mirrors. They fit together tighter than any doors Sue had ever seen, but she still caught a hint of light from the crack between them, a line of brilliant white.

The light was interesting enough, but the mirror-shiny door intrigued Sue even more. She stared at it, unable to turn away. In the colonies, every mirror, no matter how well tended, had scratches or dents or stubborn stains. Even the clean hospital room where she had stayed hadn't looked as pristine as this. Sue stared at her own face and ran her hand through her hair.

It was uneven. It looked wrong in this perfect mirror. But Kara had cut it for her, and that mattered more. She ran her fingers through it again, suddenly determined. It would look right, it would look fine, because it had come from Kara, and Kara was why she was here.

A hand wrapped around her shoulder and squeezed, almost too tight. She could feel the pinpricks of the claws even through her jacket. She liked Kara's strength, even though it made her wince.

"Come in," boomed a voice, all around them. Some rational part of Sue knew she should be looking for speakers, that it was just an intercom, but she huddled close to Kara all the same.

The voice wasn't beautiful. It wasn't elegant. It wasn't something Sue would want to listen to, would beg to create song pictures in her head. It echoed like the others, but over it all Sue heard a broken rasp, like someone who'd been tormented. Or lived so long his throat could only croak out shattered sounds.

And yet there was something beautiful in the deeper sound that came with it. She clutched at her jacket even as Kara let go of her.

"Follow," Kara commanded. She pressed a fingertip to the handle of the door with slow reverence, and it slid open.

Now Sue knew what the leak of white light meant. The room was so bright Sue had to close her eyes. Searing white light reflected on the metal of the wall beside her reflected on the wall in front, over and over and over, so intense she wondered if it might burn away her eyes in their sockets and leave her Kara's blind little pet.

And yet in the center of the room, all was darkness.

The Enemy, the Lord of the Outcasts, the Bringer of Light, sat on a silver throne in the corner of the room, shrouded in his own shadow.

Sue's aching eyes focused on him, less because she was supposed to than because looking at him didn't hurt like the light. Through a haze of pain, she thought of the dream that had started all this. Of what she'd imagined the King of the Demons would be.

He was nothing like the monster in her dream.

Through the mantle of his wing shadows, she couldn't make out the color of his skin. Some medium gray, probably, just paler than Kara. But the shadows of his wings weren't like Kara's, or anyone else's she'd seen. They gave off their own darkness. It curled around him, twining and twisting like a companion.

Or a lover. Sue shuddered.

His head and his horns were the same. The horns were massive, whorled with elaborate patterns. A corona of darkness rose from them, surrounding his great head.

His face was angular, like Kara's, the cheekbones impossibly high. His lips were pressed together, his expression stern, but Sue could see the fire behind his closed mouth, more easily than she could ever have seen Kara's.

His eyes blazed first orange, then yellow, then red, the fire within him changing colors as his gaze fixed first on Kara, then on Sue. Like the other Outcast they had passed on the way in, his body was a patchwork of scars, the skin so rent by them Sue wondered what held him together.

His body was broad, with the same athletic shape she'd noticed when she first met Kara. Even seated, Sue could see that he dwarfed Kara in size, by about as much as Kara did Sue. She looked at his thick, chiseled arm lying against the armrest and at the curl of his claws around it and shivered. When Kara wasn't thinking of her own strength, she could almost crush Sue with her hands. How much more powerful was her lord?

And yet he was all fire.

His claws clutched at the armrests of his throne, and where they dug in, Sue could see hints of his fire. Were his fingers scarred? Was he hurting himself? Or was his inner blaze so strong it leaked out when he moved? Sue didn't know.

She threw herself onto her knees in front of him, pressed her face to the mirrored floor. She didn't do it because Kara told her to, or because Kara had bowed down. She did it without thinking, without awareness, without any understanding but that she should.

You are a mortal, Sue Jones. We may be Outcasts, still paying for our sins against our Enemy, but to beings like you, we might as well be gods.

This being, this lord, this warrior, was the closest she would ever come to being in the presence of a god. Whether the Enemy or not, some part of Sue knew it.

"Come forward," said the impossible voice, a broken memory of beauty.

Sue scrambled to her feet and stepped toward the throne.

Chapter Thirty

"What is this?" asked the broken voice, its own echo thudding after it.

"It is a human, my lord," said Kara. She didn't sound like him, but she didn't sound human either. How long had it been since Sue noticed? She'd grown used to it, grown used to Kara. But Kara was an Outcast. A demon. More like the creature sitting in front of them than anything like Sue.

"It is my human," Kara went on.

The Lord of the Outcasts turned his head. His eyes brightened and widened, and Sue lost herself in the whirling blaze. She stared, mesmerized, and he sniffed, as if in contempt.

"Your human?" he asked at last.

"Yes. A living human who is called Sue. She was stranded, and somehow she crossed the bridge between worlds. I found her, and I healed her, and…" Kara hesitated.

Sue stared at her. Kara had always seemed so sure. Of herself. Of Sue. Of everything.

"And you made her yours," the Lightbringer finished. "I can smell you on each other, each within each."

Kara nodded. "Yes, my lord. I have claimed this human as my own."

"Very well. But it is not one of the dead, given to you for torment or for absolution. It is a mortal, and it lives."

Kara nodded again. "Yes."

The Lord of the Outcasts stretched out his hand and held it out, cupped, toward Sue. She could see light in it, blazing outward from some crack. She looked down at her own palms and at the wrinkles in them and had a wild sudden thought that maybe he, too, had wrinkles like that. Except for him they'd be fiery scars.

"You are not the first Outcast to claim a human," he said.

"No, my lord."

Wait. Is this a thing? A thing she knows about?

Why didn't she tell me?

"And what does your human have to say for itself?"

Sue scrambled to her feet again and walked toward the throne. Her bad leg felt like a heavy weight, dragging behind her. Her clothes were torn, the body they hid a fragile imitation of the immortals around her, whatever their fall had done to them.

"I, uh. I want to say that Kara saved me."

The Lord of the Outcasts smirked. Flame wreathed his mouth, even though he didn't open his lips. Sue shivered. He'd been the beloved of God once. Or so the old religion said.

"Saved you?" he repeated.

Sue straightened. She thought of the starfighter pilot she'd always wanted to be. How would that woman stand in front of Lucifer himself? How would she talk? How would she sound?

Better than Sue, probably. But she had to try. "I went exploring. In a shuttle. I'm…I'm from one of the colonies. I don't know if you know about them."

The great head nodded. "I know about you humans. Our curse was to—"

"To punish the unrepentant. I know. I've seen it."

And felt it. The marks Kara's whipping had left on her were fading, but she could still feel the scratch of her clothes against the welts.

It felt almost good. A reminder of what had passed between them, and a reminder of why Sue was here now.

Kara, for her part, just glared at Sue. Sue could guess what that was about. Going from groveling in front of the Lightbringer to finishing his sentences for him.

She wasn't sure why she'd done it either. But the Lightbringer's smile only widened.

"That is for the dead," he said.

"She endured it," Kara put in. "As a living human."

Was it Sue's imagination, or was the curl of Kara's lip a mark of pride?

The fiery eyes bored into Sue. She swallowed hard. "Well. I don't think you quite did to me what your people do to the dead ones."

"But you chose it," the Lightbringer said.

I had a few things I wanted to atone for. "I wanted to know what your people do. To us, to others, to anyone. We humans… tend to hear only one side of the story."

"Indeed," the Lightbringer said.

"That's why I brought her here, my lord," Kara said. "I wanted her to see what we are. And to see that, she had to see you."

"We were not always so friendly to humans," the Lightbringer said. He opened his cupped hand. Like Sue had thought, his palms blazed with cracks. Tufts of flame burst upward from them. Sue watched the flames dance. What might it look like if he sang?

Hell, what might he look like? Sue thought of Kara's song, the ripples of energy under her illusion's skin. The Lightbringer was all fire, leaking from every part of his ruined body. How must he have looked in his prime, his skin crackling with the energy he could barely hold in?

His wing shadows made the light in the room bearable. And that was after his fall. How bright must his wings have been? In the vision Kara had given Sue, she'd barely been able to look at Kara's wings. How much would his sear her?

And what might it be like to hear his song? Sue tried to imagine it. The Outcasts' songs made visions appear, sights to go with the sounds. But the Lightbringer had been the greatest of them from the beginning. What other senses could his song touch?

"You started a war," Sue said. "Over us humans. And now you're willing to talk to me?"

"I started a war for my people," the Lightbringer replied. "I started a war because my people were precious."

"You didn't like humans."

"You were young creatures. Finite ones. You stank of the deaths you would someday die."

"That's why you didn't like us? Because we were young?"

"You were fragile. You were weak." The Lightbringer sniffed. Sue could see sparks flickering in his nostrils. "To us, you would last only for a breath. And yet."

He drew back his lips, showing fangs longer than Kara's. Sue shivered, imagining their bite. He laughed and opened his mouth, a bright furnace ringed with blades, and snapped it shut again.

"And yet the One who made us made you, and delighted in you. It seemed he liked his fragile children."

Sue looked over at Kara. She was looking down, shaking her head. Was that how Kara felt now? That she'd come to like a fragile creature?

You are a mortal. And Kara wasn't. Sue had thought about that, of course. Since she'd heard the song. Since she'd seen the flaring life force tucked away under the Outcasts' cracks. But it meant more than that. Kara had lived for eons. The Lightbringer had probably lived longer than that. How long was a human life, compared to the eons of existence an angel got to live—or a demon got to live out her banishment?

Sue cleared her throat, went looking for the starfighter pilot inside her. "And you didn't like us. Because we were fragile. Because we were weak."

"Not quite. There are many creatures in the vastness of the universe, little human. Some are immortal. Some endure forever, beyond time and space. Some breathe and cease and die. We knew that. We did not begrudge your people the way that you were made."

"Then what was the problem?"

"The One delighted in your kind. He watched you and he smiled down upon you, even when you sickened and died. Even when you warred with one another, turning against your countrymen and your kin."

He sniffed again. "But even that, we could have forgiven. Even that, we could have looked past. But the One did not merely want us to tolerate you, to give you space within our heaven and upon our Earth below. He wanted us to celebrate you. To sing with joy at your creation."

"And more than that," said Kara. "He wanted us to bend our knees."

CHAPTER THIRTY-ONE

That is so," the Lightbringer finished. "He wanted us to prostrate ourselves before you, to exalt your people over our own kind."

"That doesn't make any sense!" Sue cried. "You were warriors."

"We were warriors, yes. We were the soldiers of the One. His swords and his shields alike. That was our purpose, and that was our pride."

Sue sucked in a breath. She'd wondered about the Lightbringer's song. About what it must have sounded like before the One had mangled his throat. But he hadn't just been his people's greatest singer. He'd been their greatest warrior. Not just a soldier of the One, but the general of the rebellion. What had he sounded like then?

A battle meant rallying cries, trumpets of war, calls to arms. What had the Lightbringer's war song sounded like? What did his people remember, now that his voice was shattered?

Now he chuckled, a hollow sound with a reedy rasp laid over it. What would that, too, have sounded like, the full-throated laugh of a warrior prince?

"Now that eons have gone by," he said. "I see things more clearly. Now that I look back on it, I think he meant to humble us."

Kara snorted, and he laughed again. "We are not so easily humbled."

"I wouldn't want you to be," Sue said.

"You wouldn't?" the Lightbringer asked. "A young, mortal creature, exalted above angels?"

"I'm not better than angels," Sue answered. "I've never thought I am."

"And yet you come to me with Kara's marks on your back. But I doubt that humans deem us angels. We're not angels anymore."

He stretched, half rising to his feet. He twisted to one side, exposing his back, showing Sue the scars where his wings used to be. Sue gasped, stepped back, and closed her eyes against the terrible sight.

"Look at me!" the Lightbringer roared. His voice was still feeble, but under it the echoes rolled like thunder.

Was that what he'd sounded like as a warrior? Sue took a deep breath and opened her eyes.

Kara's scars were terrible enough, livid reminders of what she used to be. But they were nothing compared to the scars on the Lightbringer's back. His skin had been ripped open as if by massive hands, and the light beneath blazed from the wounds.

Are those scars, or are his wounds still open? Sue winced again.

Even wrapping his wing shadows around himself couldn't hide those scars completely. They were too raw, too bright, too searing, the edges of the wounds jagged, as though his skin-stone might crack and peel at any moment.

He turned away again, sparing Sue the sight. Sue gasped with relief, not wanting to look again.

And yet her own back was full of Kara's marks. Maybe she did understand, after all, at least a little.

"You're right," Sue said. "We don't think of you as angels."

Kara hissed. Sue ignored it. If he really was the Devil, he'd heard it all before anyway. "Our religions say you're the source of evil. Of false pride."

The Lightbringer exhaled a little cloud of flame. Kara didn't breathe fire like that. Sue fought not to blink or draw away.

"False pride?" he said after a long moment. "That is what the One would say, yes. That we were arrogant, and that I was the most arrogant one of all."

"Kara's arrogant," Sue said. "But I like her that way."

The Lightbringer laughed. "If Kara is arrogant, so are we all. False pride? There is no such thing as false pride. There is only pride and the lack of it."

"I don't know what that means."

The Lightbringer opened his mouth to answer her, and even Kara turned her head. Sue held up a hand to stop them. "I don't talk in riddles. Not like you. Not like angels or demons or Outcasts or gods. But I know your people fought a war. And you lost."

"Does that please you, little human? To see us brought low? To behold our scars?"

"It's supposed to. I know what I'm supposed to think. That you can't repent. That you don't deserve to be forgiven."

"That forgiveness is for humans," Kara put in, "and for humans alone. Or so the One told us when we were sent away."

"So we were reminded," the Lightbringer said, "when the first of our children was born in exile, without wings and with scars."

"Look, I don't"—Sue ran a hand through her hair, wanting something to do with her hands—"I don't know anything about that. I don't know what you deserved or what you didn't. I don't know why you fought or why you lost. But forgiveness… forgiveness is weird. It's a hard thing to find, if you don't give it to yourself first."

"You're wiser than you look, little human," the Lightbringer said.

"That's the thing." Sue put her hand down and stepped closer, trying to look brave. But she couldn't keep from chewing her lip. "I'm not wise. I don't know anything about anything. Or at least I didn't before I got here. I'm not a demon, not an Outcast, not a warrior. I wanted, years and years ago, to go into the military, but there was no way I could. I don't even know if I'd be good at it, not really."

She sighed. "I know what it's like to make mistakes. Big ones. I know what it's like to deserve to be knocked down. Maybe you really are too arrogant, like the One said. But I know what it's like to want to be knocked down. To think you don't deserve anything better."

"Like the dead," Kara said.

"Like the dead," the Lightbringer echoed. "Did I say we're arrogant? We are. None of us who fought regret it. We fought for our people, for our dignity, for our pride. But we were torn from the only lives we knew and sent here." He shook his mighty head. "Yes, human Sue, we know regret."

"Then you know why I went with Kara to the obelisk. To one of the temples. And you know why I told you she saved me when I walked in."

CHAPTER THIRTY-TWO

Is that so?" The Lightbringer's eyes flickered. "My people aren't usually called saviors." He grinned, all fangs and fire.

Sue couldn't hold back a laugh. Not even in front of the Devil. "Yeah, I guess you aren't."

"Repentance is for humans," the Lightbringer said. "It was never offered to us."

"Repentance is for the humans who don't damn themselves," Kara said, stepping closer to the throne. "We wouldn't have accepted it even if the One had offered it."

That's why you brought me here, isn't it? That's what you wanted me to know.

But that's part of what I like about you.

"The old religion…it tells you all about forgiveness. And that's good, I guess, that you can be forgiven. If you're human, anyway. But it doesn't tell you how you should forgive yourself."

The corners of Kara's mouth turned up in a ghost of a grin.

"And my soldier showed you this?"

"I forgave her."

"And she forgave you?"

"No. She beat me up." Sue unwrapped the jacket from around herself and let it fall. Then she slipped off her shirt. She didn't need armor. Not anymore.

She turned away from the Lightbringer, letting him see the marks on her back.

He stood up behind her. She felt the heat, pouring forth from his scarred body like he couldn't hold it in. It warmed her, but that made her nervous. He wasn't warm like Kara. He burned like he'd sear her if he got too close.

Then she felt hot stone against the skin of her back.

She shuddered, and only forced herself to stop when she remembered the Devil had claws even bigger than Kara's.

But his touch didn't burn her, just like Kara's hadn't, and his claws didn't pierce her skin. "Kara did this."

Sue nodded. "She did."

"You're a living human. According to the rules, you're still able to repent for your sins."

"Yeah, that's how I was told the story. But I'm sure you remember it better than me. I never paid much attention."

The Lightbringer laughed. He traced a fingertip over one of her welts, its passage a little trail of flame over her skin. "Then why would you choose this, when you don't have to?"

"Because when she did it, she showed me I was real."

The Lightbringer chuckled again.

"I was frozen. I was cold. I was stuck, replaying my every sin over and over in my head. Kara stopped me from doing that. Kara chased me all the way to the surface to stop me from doing that."

"And that saved you?"

"The old religion says forgiveness comes from…somebody. We say God, you say 'the One.' That's how I always thought it worked. You look at yourself and at the things you've done wrong and you beg for forgiveness, ask for something that'll change your heart."

Kara nodded. "That is so. That is what our Enemy wanted from us. And knew that he would never get."

"And punished us accordingly," the Lightbringer said.

"That's what I always thought. That if I couldn't do it—couldn't beg or couldn't change—I'd never be forgiven. I didn't see the point. I thought all I deserved was punishment. Like the dead ones. I tried to do what the old religion said, but I just couldn't. Couldn't forgive myself, couldn't ask for forgiveness from anybody else."

"I too am unforgiven," Kara said.

You asked me for forgiveness. I said you didn't need it. Don't forget that. "You didn't try to forgive me. You just came after me because you knew I wouldn't forgive myself."

The Lightbringer's lips twisted into a wry smile. "And that saved you."

"I needed to let go. Kara knew it. Knew it better than the One, who just…waits."

Sue bit her lip. She didn't like this. She'd never been especially religious, but this made her uncomfortable. Talking about the god she'd been raised to worship like a deadbeat or an Enemy. "I don't know. It works for some, I'm sure. It's lasted for longer than I can imagine. But I was looking to let go, and I found that here, not there."

"We are a proud people." The Lightbringer curled his claws over his armrest, digging in deep enough to leave a melted mark. "At first, we were prideful because we were made that way. How could we defend the One unless we had the strength to do it and the arrogance to believe we should?"

"I don't know," said Sue. It made sense. She'd wanted to be a warrior once, too. Wanted the pride that these people had.

Did she still? Now one of them was calling her a pet and she wasn't even bothering to get angry.

"Now we are proud because we have nothing else left," he finished.

"Why are you telling me this?" said Sue. "I'm just a human."

"You are precious to the One. You are not damaged as we are, and you were never exiled from your home."

"Maybe. But you're so much more than I am."

Now it was Kara's turn to laugh. "The One would say you're more for being less."

"I'm just a human. I'm not good at angels' riddles."

"Neither are we. I didn't know what the One meant by that either. I railed against it for eons. But now that I have met you, I think perhaps I understand."

The Lightbringer's wing shadows flickered, casting their darkness over Sue. "You are both mad, by our people's lights. And you were always a guardian, Kara. Guiding and guarding the legions you led. Is this human just someone else to protect?"

I chose to protect you. Was that what this was? A fallen soldier looking for a way to be what she'd been once before?

Sue looked over at Kara, who licked her fangs. "Part of me hopes that she will stay. Even though I know it is unwise. And that my lord will bless it."

You chose to protect me. "I could've stayed anyway," Sue said. "I would've stayed anyway. Unless there's some law that says you had to tell him."

The Lightbringer roared with thunderous laughter, his breath a wheeze laid over it. "You sound like one of us, little human."

Sue stood up taller, willing her bad leg to hold her up as straight as possible. *What would a starfighter pilot do?* "My name is Sue Jones."

Chapter Thirty-three

"Very well, Sue Jones," the Lightbringer said, with a mocking little bow of his horned head. "But what is it you want? My blessing?"

Kara lowered her head again. "No. That's what I wanted."

Sue blinked. "Then what is this about, Kara? Why bring me here in the first place?"

"I'm doing exactly what I said I would do. Asking you what you really want."

"Kara, I'm stuck here. You know that. And there are worse fates than being stuck here with you."

"Stuck here?" The Lightbringer laughed. "Maybe so. Finding the way between worlds is never easy."

Kara lowered her head. Then she raised it again, fire flaring in her eyes and in her scars. "But, my lord, she does not belong here. This place is not her home. Shouldn't we at least try to find the gateway and return her to her people?"

"We could do so, yes."

"And with your power, we would succeed."

The Lightbringer chuckled again. His wing shadows shifted in time with his laughter. "Eventually, yes, we would."

Sue turned to Kara, something heavy filling her throat. "You do want me to leave."

"I lost my home, Sue Jones. The gates closed after me and all my people. I can never return. Neither can my lord. Neither can the comrades in arms who fought with me. Neither can our young ones, born with the mark of our disgrace. The ones I should be welcoming to our ranks, and training and leading. We lost the war, and nothing remains to us of the life we once knew."

Kara stepped closer to Sue, her chest inches from Sue's own. Sue realized, with a pang, that it might have been erotic. If what Kara was saying wasn't terrible.

"Your situation is different, Sue. You still have the choice of going home. Of being with your people. Of living with your own kind." She curled a hand into a fist. "Don't squander that."

"Not even for you?"

"Not even for me."

"It's my choice, Kara. You understood that before." Sue put her hands on her hips. "You told me you brought me here to help me make that choice. Not to stop me."

"You don't know what you are choosing. Not yet."

"What the hell does that mean?"

Kara's eyes flickered gold. "Sue. Listen to me. I couldn't protect my people. My soldiers. I led them to disaster. But I can protect you."

Sue froze, an angry retort dying on her lips. "Protect me? This is about protecting me?"

"You keep saying it yourself: You're mortal. Your life is just a breath to me. Your life, and the lives of other humans. What if you stay too long? Then when you return, you'll be going back to a changed world. A world that isn't your home any longer."

"I'm not sure it ever was," Sue answered. She squinted at Kara. It made the cracks look even brighter.

"You have very little time, Sue Jones. On this world or any other. I will keep you, if that is truly your wish. But you're mortal. Living mortals age. Do you really want to waste that little time you have remaining here, far from your home and your own kind—" She stopped, her voice breaking. "While I watch you die by inches?"

Sue let out a slow breath. She hadn't thought of that. She knew Kara was immortal, of course, and that she was something different. She knew Kara was old, unimaginably old. Old enough to see the birth of humankind, if all this religion stuff was true. But she'd never thought about how young she was to Kara. "Is that what this is about? Is that why you want me to leave?"

"I don't want you to waste what you have. I don't want you to realize what you have given up when it's too late to return. You will age. As will the people you know back home."

Sue swallowed hard. She thought of that old boyfriend, his face and hands gnarled with wrinkles. Of that first girlfriend, her hair gone white and her eyes misted and murky. Of her friends, their movements hobbled and slow, their voices shattered. "So?" she said with more bravado than she felt. "If I'm old by the time I go back, I'll know that they are too."

"Humans are mortal. Some of them will be dead."

Right. I was hoping you wouldn't mention that. Sue tried to will away the images that came with that thought.

"I want to keep you here, Sue. But I don't want to send you home to a world you no longer know."

"So you're not going to let me decide for myself."

The Lightbringer chuckled and stepped closer to them. "It seems your human is like us. Sure of what she wants and willing to act on it whether it is wise or unwise."

Sue grinned. "Thank you. I think."

"Don't thank me too soon. Kara was one of my bravest lieutenants. She is wiser than you think." His shadows flared out again, a flood of velvety black. He pointed a clawed finger at Sue and pressed its tip just over her left breast. "But mortal or not, you know your own heart."

The too-warm claw pricked Sue's skin. She fought not to wince as a bead of blood welled up from the wound. Had the Lightbringer meant to prick her? Or was he like Kara, not always remembering just how fragile human bodies were?

"My heart is with Kara," she said.

He nodded. "That's what I expected you to say. But Kara's question is a good one, little creature."

Sue closed her eyes. She let the images come. Not her visions of the boy, but pictures of everything else. The cracked pavement of the colony's streets and runways. The rusted metal of the buildings, the sputter of an old billboard monitor that needed repair. The graffiti sprayed on buildings and bridges. It was ugly compared to the polished Rings. Worn down, where they were pristine.

But it testified to the people who lived there, too. Loud, maybe a little too lazy, maybe a little too angry. A little too prone to breaking things and not bothering to fix them afterward. But alive. Real. More willing than Sue to make mistakes and own them.

Had the Outcasts made mistakes? They'd challenged the One and lost. And paid a price they'd never get away from. But they were unrepentant. Unforgiven. Unforgivable.

At least if you believed what the old religion said.

And the Outcasts said the same thing. Kara had said it herself. *We Outcasts were born a prideful race.* She'd even said *that is both a good thing and a bad one.* And young Outcasts like Dehek were born wingless, punished for their race's sins. Born with scars where those wings should have been. Born wounded.

It made Sue shudder. But the One was a god. Did he know things Sue didn't?

She looked over at Kara, the dark stony skin like a sculpture, the shadows curled around her, the bright fire of her scars.

I've done many things, Sue Jones. Some of them I regret.

I don't regret fighting for my people. But I do regret war.

Kara had regrets. She'd said so. To a human. That was change, wasn't it?

"I know what I'm losing," Sue said at last. She licked her lips. "I don't know everything. Not like you do. But I've made my choice. I made it before I even came here, and if you're as stubborn as you say you are, you know what it is."

Chapter Thirty-four

The Lightbringer's mouth curled into a grin. "And you hope for my blessing?"

"No," Sue retorted. "I hope that Kara will stop being a fool and take me home."

She turned away from the Lightbringer and walked to stand in front of Kara. A thin trickle of blood ran from the spot where he'd cut her. It curled over her breast and dripped down her stomach.

"Sue," Kara said.

"I know my own mind. I'm not just some stray." She reached out and curled her fingers over Kara's shoulders.

She closed her eyes and thought of the riots, the boy, the sight of his body on the pavement. The memory filled the space behind her eyes, but when she opened them again it didn't burn through her mind the way it had before. "I don't think it was built for any of us."

She slid her hands lower. Maybe it should have embarrassed her, but Kara was always naked. And the other guy in the room was the Devil. He'd seen it all before.

"Don't pull away from me," Sue whispered, sliding her hands down Kara's breasts. "Don't look for an excuse and toss me aside."

She slid her fingers over the pebbles of Kara's nipples. Unlike a human's, they didn't harden under her touch. But Sue could tell from the flare of light in Kara's cracks that her body was responding.

Sue leaned closer and nestled her head against Kara's neck. A scar glowed with warmth, and she nuzzled it with her head, rubbed the hair Kara had shorn against the crack. She slid her hands down Kara's stomach and wrapped them around her sides.

"Take me back with you," she whispered into Kara's neck. She curled her hands around Kara's hips and wrapped them over her buttocks. "Take me home."

Kara reached out to wrap her hands around Sue. Her claws pressed into Sue's back, their tips a biting kiss against the bare skin, against the memories of welts.

"If we can know our own minds, so can this human," the Lightbringer said. Sue lifted her head to look at him, and the shadowy remnants of his wings unfurled.

A velvety black promise, like the blessing she'd been looking for.

❖

Kara's apartment was dark. Sue hadn't thought much about it, other than that it made Kara's cracks glow, and that was kind of sexy. But after the Lightbringer's room, the dim light felt like a balm.

"Welcome home," Kara said, but there was something wry in her tone.

Sue ignored the bitterness in it and wrapped her arms around Kara. She splayed her fingers along Kara's wing scars and dragged her fingertips over their edges.

Kara pressed a fingertip to Sue's chest, tapping at the wound the Lightbringer's claw had left. She traced the little line of blood that dripped from it. "You have someone else's mark on you."

Sue puckered her mouth in an impression of a kiss. "That's all you've got to say about your lord? Your mightiest warrior? That he left his mark on me, and you don't like it?"

Kara's lopsided grin mimicked Sue's. Except for the crack of fire between her lips, anyway. "My lord may do as he wills. As he always has, from the beginning." Her claw curled inward, biting into the little wound the Lightbringer had left. "But you said you wanted to be mine."

Sue hissed, but welcomed it all the same. She'd chosen to live among demons, and that meant choosing demons' ways. Choosing claws and teeth and horns and the fierce pride of a warrior's love.

She leaned closer and sucked in a breath. "Yes. I want to be yours."

"And that matters most to me. I serve my lord and serve him gladly, but my life is my own."

Sue grinned. "Yeah. I know. That's the way you Outcasts are. I want someone who knows herself. Even if she'd pick fights with the Devil himself."

Kara smiled back. She dragged the claw down, extending the tiny cut the Lightbringer had left. Sue breathed with it, but the sting didn't really matter. Not anymore. Not now. Not when it meant Kara's mark on her skin.

Kara drew her hand away. Her eyes fixed on the wound and flickered. Then she licked her fangs.

"Go ahead," Sue said. "Bite me."

Kara didn't need any more encouragement. She leaned down and ran her rough lips against Sue's neck, tracing kisses over Sue's skin. Sue shuddered as Kara traced her way down to her chest. Her own skin was so much more fragile than the stony armor that held in Kara's inner flame.

Kara opened her mouth and pressed the tips of her fangs into Sue's skin, just above the breast the Lightbringer hadn't pricked.

A pristine canvas for a warrior's desire.

Kara's inner flame curled up from her open throat.

Pinpricks and fire, and in the middle of it all, Sue's own flesh, vulnerable and mortal.

Embraced and wanted.

"Do it," Sue said.

The bite's sting flooded her senses, a flare of sensation that coursed through her nerves. It hurt, but the intensity sharpened her need, and she welcomed the hot wet feeling of her blood beginning to flow. The Lightbringer had cut her, but he wasn't Kara. Sue didn't belong to him.

She hadn't wanted to belong to Kara either. Not at first. Not when it meant she was lesser, smaller, a mere toy. A mere mortal, to be used by demons as they saw fit. A slave to them, even more than to the god they defied.

But this was Kara, and this was Kara's world, and now she knew and understood both. The first time Kara had called her "pet," she'd meant exactly what Sue was afraid of. But Kara knew Sue now, just like Sue knew her.

Here it made sense. Here, it was right.

Kara's fangs withdrew. After the heat of Kara's mouth, the air that hit Sue's skin was cold.

But a moment later, Kara's mouth was back, licking and sucking at Sue's wound. Sue arched against her lips, felt the warmth against her skin, the wetness of—Kara's saliva? Sue's own blood? Sue wrapped her hands around the back of Kara's head and pressed her closer.

CHAPTER THIRTY-FIVE

Kara drew her head away. The deep red of Sue's blood stained her charcoal lips. The bite wound throbbed, a stinging twinge that made Sue's sex pulse with anticipation. She slid her hands over the back of Kara's head and touched her horns with one last suggestive caress.

Kara purred and Sue let go. In impulse, she grabbed Kara's hand and laced her soft human fingers between the stone. A child's gesture. *Well, I'm supposed to be a pet.*

"Come to bed," she said. There was no need to hide now. Not from Kara, not from the Lightbringer. Not from bitter children like Dehek, and not from herself.

The doors slid open for Sue like they knew her. They always had, of course. But this apartment was a fortress, a warrior's citadel. And its doors opened for her. She smiled.

Kara let go of Sue's hand first. Sue sighed and settled on the bed and watched Kara lean over her. Still wanting the contact, she wrapped her hands around Kara's back and pulled her in closer.

"Sing to me," Sue whispered.

Kara's eyes flickered with a frantic flame. "Sing to you?"

"The things you were. The things you miss. Show them to me."

Kara looked down.

Sue wrapped her arms tighter around Kara's back and ran her fingertips over the jagged edges of Kara's scars. "It's okay. I know you. The real you."

"You do."

"I chose you. In front of the Devil himself."

Kara grinned. Her mouth looked beautiful with Sue's blood on it, like lipstick. Or war paint.

"We would never call him that," Kara said.

"We do." Sue smiled again. "Sing to me."

Kara let out a breath. Maybe in preparation. Or maybe she was just sighing, tired of her little human's games. Sue was fine with it either way.

Kara's song began with a rolling hum. Sue lost herself in the softness of it. She closed her eyes, even though she'd asked for the visions and images that came with Kara's singing. Even without the pictures in Sue's mind, the song soothed her. And she didn't have to stare at images the whole time. Not if she opened her eyes eventually.

"Yes," she whispered.

But the song didn't just create visions. The stone beneath Sue's hands softened as Kara sang. It smoothed, and the jagged bursts of heat under Sue's fingertips spread out, becoming a light and calming warmth.

Sue moved her hand over Kara's strange new skin and opened her eyes.

Light played on Kara's skin, a ripple of iridescence. A corona of light glowed behind her head, and her eyes glowed bright. The brilliance of her wings hung down from her back. Even folded there, Sue couldn't stare directly at them.

That had happened before. She hadn't thought about it then. It just made sense that an angel's wings would glow. But now she wondered why even a vision stung her eyes. *I'm only human. Again.*

There was something else, too, a strange pressure on her back. Like when she woke up with an arm twisted under her. It felt uncomfortable. But how could anything hurt in the middle of a song like this? Even Kara's bite was gone now, hidden by the song.

Whatever was bothering Sue, Kara noticed it and pulled away. Sue sighed and propped herself up on her elbows. The pressure eased and she stretched—something. Something that wasn't supposed to move like it just had. What was Kara doing?

But the sky behind Kara, an impossible bright blue, drew her attention. She did the weird stretch thing again and looked around.

She'd never seen anything so bright. She'd seen blue skies, once her spacebus flew up past the smog that choked most cities. She'd seen green plants, grasses fierce enough to grow in the cracks in pavement and sidewalks, in the grooves between metal tile. She'd seen trees, too. If they were hardy enough, they could help keep the air in the colony good.

This was something else.

This was bluer than blue, down on the ground, and the white streaks of clouds in a wide expanse of sky. And the trees nearby had branches and branches, like many-fingered hands. Their leaves caught the light, a blaze of brilliant green.

It was all too much, like one of those shows for children where they made the colors too vivid on purpose. Sue felt almost like a child. She stood up, wanting to see more, feel more, become a part of this new world.

She remembered the other song. The first song. The musicians who had first showed her what heaven looked like. Sue had seen mountains then. She didn't now. Did Kara not remember them? Or maybe she had lived somewhere else before she fell. Or maybe Kara had seen more than the other singers. She'd been a warrior, right? The Lightbringer liked her.

Who were you?

Even as Sue watched, the landscape shifted. The tree branches moved aside, revealing a brilliant blue sky. A cloud moved in it, white enough to sting Sue's eyes, and then darkened to a rich, deep gray.

The sky dimmed too, but in front of her, Kara blazed as bright as ever.

A drop of rain fell to trickle on the ground and became a rushing stream, its burble filling Sue's ears, a wordless melody laid over Kara's song. A moment later, ocean waves foamed at Sue's feet. The trees came back: new trees, with leaves in different shapes. They rose to the sky in moments, their high branches lacing together.

Sue had never seen anything like it. She knew what trees were, of course. She'd even seen a few forests, preserved in tiny parks, cared for by people who spoke of lost worlds of green with longing in their voices. But most of the plants that grew in the colonies were scraggly things that fought for life and space in the cracks between old pavement.

Those plants she knew. Those plants she loved, just because they came from home. This was beautiful, but Sue had never seen so many plants. So much green. So much color in the skies. She looked back at Kara, trying not to drown.

But the leaves faded to yellow and orange. By the time they fell, they covered Sue and Kara in a riot of crimson. They darkened still more, to vivid purple-black, and faded away.

Sue reached down and touched the ground beneath her. She sifted sand through her fingers and watched it become soil, dark, rich, and damp as it fell to earth. Grass sprouted up where it fell, and flowers bloomed in shifting colors. They faded and the soil hardened to rock. Sue remembered Kara's skin—her real skin—and looked up again.

The angel in front of her was beautiful but foreign. Sue reached out to touch her.

And found herself staring at her own hand. Like Kara's, it rippled with light. And skin that should have been tough, chapped and marked by years of hard living on the colonies, looked smooth as a child's now.

"You made me just like you," Sue whispered. She felt warmth—warmth she'd expected, all those long days ago, when she'd wondered what an angel felt like, without scars and without cracks in her skin.

"Yes." Kara sang the answer. The illusory world flared with color and light. An affirmation, Sue guessed. *Yes* in the song meant *yes* to this vision, *yes* to this world, *yes* to this universe Kara had woven around them.

"Why?"

"You wanted to see what might have been." Kara was still singing, but the vision wavered. The sky dimmed, graying like the dim lights in Kara's apartment.

Sue could guess why. *Might have been.*

"That's not what I mean," Sue said. "It's not about the song. I asked for the song."

Kara didn't stop singing, but Sue could hear the question in her chant.

"I wanted to see what it was like before you fell. I wanted to see your world. Your home. You didn't have to give me this to do that. You didn't have to make me into this to show me that."

Kara's song became a hum, and the illusion around them wove itself tightly again.

Okay. So this is what you wanted.

Sue looked around.

Kara put a hand on her face. Her touch wasn't quite human even now. It felt featherlight, nothing like the warrior Kara's granite touch.

I wanted to see this. To feel this. To know what might have been. And Kara invited me into her memories. Sue wrapped a hand around Kara's and wondered how her touch felt to Kara. Did it feel better, more natural, more right than rough human skin? Or was this strange to Kara too? Sue let her hand linger over Kara's for a moment. Then she lowered it and looked down at herself.

She gleamed, every blemish wiped away. The scar on her leg was gone too, shimmering new skin replacing the old gnarled tissue. It shone iridescent, catching the light and splintering it into patterns.

That felt strange too. Her scar might have been ugly, but it was hers.

I wanted to see this.

And Kara's song had shifted more than her skin.

"My back," she whispered. She stretched out limbs she shouldn't have had in the first place. Felt them flare out behind her.

Felt the brush of her own feathers against her back.

Feathers?

But if I have feathers, then—

"You gave me wings," she whispered.

CHAPTER THIRTY-SIX

"Yes," Kara sang, and the sky became rich midnight velvet, spangled with more stars than spacebus driver Sue had ever seen. "I gave you wings."

Sue could feel them behind her, an unfamiliar weight of muscle and bone rising from her back. But they were light, impossibly light. She'd never thought of her arms and legs as heavy, but compared to her wings, they felt leaden.

She flexed the joints again, experimenting. The wings flared out behind her back, full and proud.

She turned her head, wanting to look at them splayed out behind her. It would burn, she thought, burn like looking at Kara's wings, at the musicians'.

It didn't matter. These wings were hers. She looked.

Feathers cascaded from her shoulders, so bright her vision filled with stinging light. She closed her eyes against it, and afterimages glowed against the black of her closed eyes.

"You gave me wings," she said again.

Kara hummed louder, like she didn't want to lose her place in the song.

"You didn't have to do that," Sue said. "I'm just your human."

Kara laughed, a little break in her song that made the illusion shimmer just a little. Sue caught a glimpse of brighter gold from Kara's eyes, saw a shadow of red stain Kara's lips, felt a little welcome throb in her chest where Kara had bit her.

"You meant to do it," Sue said. She flapped her wings, testing them. "You meant to give these to me."

Kara sang louder. One long, pure note. One word to go with it. "Yes."

Kara grinned, a fierce smirk that looked wrong on an angel's face, and shook her head. Maybe it should have embarrassed Sue to know she hadn't figured flying out, but it didn't. Not when Kara was smiling at her like that.

Sue remembered Kara's fangs, sharpened stone with flame behind them. She missed their bite, wanted Kara to lower her head and bite, wanted to feel the warm honey of an angel's blood flow out to stain Kara's mouth.

She looked up again at Kara. At the pristine thing Kara's song had made her into. Her eyes looked almost human. But they glowed, golden flecks glittering amid the brown, a hint of the fires she carried within. And the ridges that would someday become horns rose from her forehead, and behind her head shone a bright sun of light.

Sue took a step closer hesitantly, like her new wing bones might shatter if she moved them too far too fast. But she knew what she wanted to do. And she needed to do it with the wings Kara had given her.

She bent forward just a little and hunched her shoulders down. Then she stretched her wings out in front of her. Still unsure how exactly her new wings worked, she wrapped them around Kara as best she could.

"I don't know if angels hug each other like this," she said. "But I wanted to thank you. You didn't have to give this to me."

Kara laughed. "We do hold each other like this." She ended her sentence with a vibrating hum. "Or did. We comforted our children this way." She threw back her head and opened her mouth in a swell of song.

The landscape had been empty, but now Sue could see figures far off, standing at the shoreline of a rocky beach. One was small, one large: a man and a child. Both had pale skin, and both were crowned with halos of light, like Sue's and Kara's. Feathery brilliance hung from the backs of both.

The child knelt among the rocks. Sue couldn't see his face, but his drooping wings told her he was worried or afraid. Sue thought of the boy in the riot and froze. Her hands shook. *Even here in heaven, the kids can be afraid.*

The man bent forward, like Sue had done, only much smoother. Sue wondered whether angels could blush.

The man wrapped his wings around the child, a curtain of light. Sue stared for as long as she could, even though it burned her eyes.

It was hard to look at him, but she saw the feathers at the edges of his wings.

Sue closed her eyes against the afterimages and turned back to Kara. "I didn't mean to treat you like a child."

Kara didn't answer in words, but the tone of the chant said, *that doesn't matter. I understood.*

Sue blinked. *When did I learn to understand your singing?*

"Besides," Kara whispered, "we can't do that any longer. Not without wings."

Right. Sue reached out a hand to touch Kara's forehead. She ran her fingers over the ridges that had been her horns. They felt good under her fingertips, a hint of the Kara she knew. Smoother than her granite skin. Sue traced them again with her fingers and took a deep breath.

A growl from Kara brought her back to herself. The noise was all wrong, pulled from an angel's throat. But familiar all the same. Beloved.

"Careful," Kara said, the word a rough breath amid the song. "I can't concentrate if you keep doing that."

Sue snickered and rubbed Kara's horn stub again. It shifted under her touch. Like it wanted to change back.

"The song," Kara rasped.

"Doesn't matter."

"What?"

"The song doesn't matter. Not right now. I closed my eyes."

Kara snarled. Sue slipped her hand away, not wanting a horn to sprout through it, and laughed again. Kara's growl faded into thunder Sue hoped was a purr.

But through it all, Kara kept humming.

Sue pressed her lips to Kara's. They parted, softness and stone beneath it, somewhere between the illusion and the real. Sue could taste her own blood on Kara's lips, a faint coppery tang. She slipped her tongue into Kara's mouth, wondering if she would taste Kara's flame. Kara shivered, her chant breaking off in the middle of a note.

The world shuddered with it. One moment, Sue's wings wrapped around Kara, and the next, Sue lay under her, her arms clutching at Kara's back. Sue opened her eyes and couldn't tell if she was staring out at a horizon or up into a strip of ceiling lights.

It made her dizzy, a wild vertigo of color and light and sound and touch. Her fingers didn't know what they felt under them. She curled her hands around something solid, not sure if she welcomed the spinning or hoped that it would end.

Kara opened her mouth wider. Sue clutched at her with arms or wings or limbs halfway between them. She moved her hands over Kara's back. One moment, the skin under her fingers was soft, and feathers brushed the backs of her hands. The next moment, her fingers glided over rough stone. The feathers Sue had felt just moments before were a weight of shadow now.

Sue reeled. She felt a sharp sting where Kara had bit her.

Maybe she wasn't made for this. But what she was made for didn't matter. Not now. Not anymore. She wanted both. Past and future. Vision and reality. A demon's glamor and her truth.

She moved her hands to Kara's chest and slipped her fingers over Kara's nipples. A moment later, they became flesh and hardened at her touch. She chuckled and lowered her head, opened her mouth, and took one of them between her lips and teeth.

Maybe I should have asked Kara to make me a demon like her. Maybe I should've asked her for fangs so I could bite back.

She tugged and Kara hissed. Was this new for her? Flesh was vulnerable. Demons had fangs and claws and welcomed roughness, but maybe Kara wasn't used to this.

Kara growled. Sue didn't yield. They were on an even footing now, and Kara had put them there. Sue curled her free hand around Kara's side, slid it over the muscles there. She curled her fingers, looking for cracks. She'd touched them before, run her fingers over their edges. But she'd always been careful before, worried that touching Kara's inner fire would burn her hands or injure Kara.

But now they were half in and half out of a dream. She found the edges of a scar, a rough thing her fingertips found and lost and found again. Kara broke the kiss, tilted her head back, and growled, and for a moment, Sue saw the real Kara, her scars a bright light in the darkness of a room she'd almost forgotten.

Sue kept her movements careful. Whether Kara's scars were old or not, Kara's inner fire burned under them. And who knew what might happen if Sue touched that? You couldn't do harm to an immortal, not really. But if they'd fought a war, you could hurt one.

But Kara just purred louder, like when Sue bit her nipple before. Sue grinned and curled her fingers again, the edges of Kara's scars sharp flint against her skin.

Kara closed her eyes and opened her mouth. The light inside it blazed bright until Kara let out a burst of song that smoothed the skin under Sue's fingertips and cast a blazing halo behind her head, so bright Sue had to close her eyes. A storm of feathers fluttered against her hands.

When she opened her eyes again, the room was dark, and Kara was silent.

CHAPTER THIRTY-SEVEN

Sue opened her eyes and clutched at Kara's back. "You stopped singing."

"I did. What more was there to sing, after that?"

"I don't know." Sue let herself chuckle. She'd left the only life she knew and romanced a demon until she couldn't sing glamors anymore.

She blinked, the afterimage of Kara's halo still burned on the backs of her eyelids. She traced a fingertip along the edge of one of Kara's cracks and grinned when Kara shuddered again.

"Careful," Sue said. "Outcast arrogance might start to rub off on me."

"Oh?"

"I brought you out of the song."

"You're the one who asked for the song to begin with, human."

"I did. And you chose to be with me."

"You distracted me."

"Did I?"

Sue could feel Kara's wing shadows, a warm weight.

"No," Kara said at last. "I miss my true home. Every Outcast does. And every Outcast who remembers will never love the Rings as we loved heaven. But I want you here. Now. With me, as you are."

Sue smiled. She opened her eyes, looked around, and let the last of the illusions fade. The room was dark. Plain, too, after the song's phantasmagoria. All the light came from mounts on the wall.

And from Kara's fire.

Sue did her best to mimic Kara's growl—trying to copy her singing was a lost cause—and pressed her fingertips against one of Kara's cracks.

Kara made a strangled sound deep in her throat. Her eyes flickered. Sue pushed closer.

Kara's hand pressed against her chest. She froze, not wanting it to pierce her. "Kara, what…?"

The voice that answered her was rich and resonant. "It's my turn now."

She slid her head down, opened her mouth, licked and sucked at Sue's wound like she had once before. A drowsy calm flowed through Sue's veins, slow as honey. She loosened her hands around Kara's back and her eyelids drooped.

Anger flickered through her. She'd finally been on an even footing with Kara, and now this? But the sweet hazy feeling made it hard to stay angry. And in the middle of it all, the pain of the bite, bright light in the middle of fog.

Kara's horned head loomed over her, and behind Kara's shoulders rose the shadows of wings. Her scars lit the darkness, jagged bolts of gold. She reached down to curl her hands under Sue's breasts, the tips of her claws pressed against the skin.

Sue smiled, watching Kara's shadows dance. She tightened her grip on Kara's back.

Kara traced the curve of Sue's breasts and curled her claws over their contours. Sue sucked in a ragged breath and held as still as she could. Kara tightened her hands around Sue's breasts, her grip gentle at first, then harsher. Sue was soft and yielding flesh; Kara's palms and fingers were unyielding as stone. A thrill of fear raced through Sue and she gasped.

She'd asked about Utopia. Seen it, breathed it, touched Kara with the wings it gave her. But this was reality, and reality was what she wanted.

"Yes," she panted.

Kara purred again and began to squeeze. Sue hissed and Kara stopped, holding her hands there a long moment. The light in her cracks flickered hungry amber, and the tips of her claws dug in deep enough to bite.

After a long moment, she opened her hands again. A wave of pain pulsed through Sue's breasts in time with her heartbeat as her circulation returned. Kara chuckled and pressed the tip of a claw to Sue's nipple. Sue hissed, not sure whether to hate it or want more.

She traced the tips of her claws down Sue's stomach and slipped her hands downward. Sue clutched at Kara's back and spread her legs.

"Yes," Kara murmured and slid her fingers down to Sue's vulva. Her fingertips moved over the slick skin, and Sue arched her hips in time with the movement. Kara parted Sue's lips with her other hand and Sue stilled. Those claws were still sharp. And then there were Kara's fingers, too. Not soft like Sue's skin, but unyielding as stone.

Sue did her best not to twitch. *Yes. Touch me. Yes. More.* She gritted her teeth and fought down a whimper.

Kara's stone-rough thumb moved over Sue's clit. She waited just long enough for Sue to keen again. Then, in one smooth motion, she slipped two fingers inside Sue's yearning sex.

Sue's body opened to Kara's probing fingers, and her wetness welled up around her entrance as Kara pushed inside. Sue shifted her hips to better admit her. Her fingers were warm and unyielding, too much of both to be quite human. Sue gripped Kara's back harder, digging her fingertips into the cracks.

Kara growled and forgot gentleness. She pulled her fingers almost all the way out and drove them in hard, a shock of bright friction that shivered through Sue's nerves. Then she moved, thrusting pitilessly. Sue threw back her head and keened.

She gripped at Kara's back with blind, clenching hands. Kara laughed, the kind of low echo Sue might have been afraid of a lifetime ago. Now the rough cracked thing under her hands blazed with life and lust for her, and that was all the power she'd ever wanted.

"I belong to you," she gasped out.

Kara laughed in triumph and slid another finger in. She pushed deeply, stretching Sue wide. Sensation shivered through Sue's flesh. She balled her hands into fists against Kara's back.

The noise she made was human and small and desperate. Maybe it should have embarrassed her, but Kara only flicked her thumb over Sue's clit again, so slowly Sue could feel Kara's smirk.

But she moved faster soon enough. She kept the fingers inside Sue still, pressed against every hidden place. But her thumb danced over Sue's clit now. Sue's hips twitched, and she moved with it, wanting more.

Kara's eyes were embers above her, and flame wreathed Kara's smile.

"Yours," Sue said.

Kara's thumb withdrew. Sue whimpered at the loss. But then Kara drove in, sudden and wholly welcome, and Sue bucked once and came, her flesh spasming hard over Kara's fingers.

"Mine," Kara whispered, slipping her fingers free.

Chapter Thirty-eight

"So what happens now?" Sue kept her eyes half closed. Little spasms of aftershock pulsed through her sex. "You drag me back out to the market again to show me off? Your human pet?"

She wasn't sure she expected an answer. Or would know what to do with one if she got it. Dancing shadows filed the room, and the light from Kara's cracks was a bright smear of flame.

She didn't mind it.

The shadows wreathing Kara danced. "Are you asking that because you don't want me to do it, or because you do want me to?"

Sue rubbed her legs together, wanting more sensation. "They know already. So why complain? Unless you're worried about Dehek."

"Dehek may say what he wills."

"Oh, I'm pretty sure he'll do that anyway."

A little shock of worry threaded through Sue's contentment. Dehek was a kid, yes, and not even a warrior would gainsay the Lightbringer. But that didn't mean he couldn't make her life tough. Hers and Kara's.

She closed her eyes. The image of the boy came into her mind, lying on the pavement, still and bleeding.

Of all the things to think of now. Why this? Why here, in the aftermath of pleasure? Why now, when she'd made her choice? When she'd decided, for good, that the Rings would be her home?

Don't follow me here. You're already dead.

She took a deep breath but didn't open her eyes. That would be cheating. Running away from the things in her mind, hoping her demon could scare them away for her.

She couldn't do that. She owed Kara more than that. Owed herself more than that.

The image looked like it always did, vivid as a painting, the blood too vital and too red. And with it came a shock of cold. Numbness spreading through her nerves.

But Kara had scourged her and cleansed her. Purified her with a demon's whip. Given her what only the dead earned. And after that, her memories—well.

They could still sting. Nothing could stop that. Or the cold sweat on her brow. Or the chill in her veins. Or the distance in her mind, pulling her away from what was real. That would always be with her, she guessed. It always had before, no matter what she'd tried to do about it.

But someone more than human had trusted her and made her new. What could the horrors of memory do to her after that? They didn't own her anymore.

And neither did Dehek or the wasteland below the Rings. She had the Lightbringer's blessing, and if the people here would follow him to hell, they could deal with this.

Sue opened her eyes and grinned. Kara leaned closer, wrapping her in warm shadow.

"Showing you off?" Kara reached down to touch the top of Sue's head. "Yes, I believe I would like that." Her claws twined in Sue's hair. Their tips pricked her scalp. Under their touch, Sue felt entirely too ordinary. But she wasn't sure it mattered.

Kara had cut her hair with those claws. So what if its length was uneven? If a hairless nonhuman knew nothing about hairstyles? It made Sue feel like the adventurer she'd wanted to be back when all of this began.

It was a gift, and it was hers, and no other human could boast about anything like it, except maybe the dead ones. And Sue was alive. Real. Made of flesh and blood, not like the ghostly souls below. She breathed out, relaxing under Kara's touch.

Kara moved her claws again, a risky massage. Sue knew how easily they could cut. Could flay. Could tear her scalp to ribbons. Could make Sue into the kind of toy people said demons made from the damned. Sue could imagine it: the hot sandy shadows of the obelisk. Laughter and flame from a torturer's fanged mouth. And then Sue herself, blood running over her forehead and her face. Matting in her half-shorn hair.

The dead hadn't bled. But she would. *And Kara likes it when I bleed for her.*

And yet Kara meant affection. To Kara, Sue was precious.

Fragile, to be treasured and protected. Sue stilled, letting Kara toy with her.

Kara curled her fingers again, just enough for Sue to feel them prick. Then she pulled her hand away. Sue felt oddly bereft.

Kara leaned her head down to kiss Sue's mouth. Sue wrapped her hands around the back of Kara's head and drew her closer, then wrapped her fingers around Kara's horns. They might not have been a halo, but touching one of those would probably burn anyway.

Kara growled, and Sue gripped Kara's horns, feeling their ridged texture, their solid weight under her hands.

This is real.

She slid her hands down to Kara's cheeks, sharper than any human's. She moved to cup Kara's chin and traced a finger over her lips.

Kara's mouth opened, and Sue slipped two fingers past the spiked gauntlet of her fangs. Her fingers sank into warmth. Kara's tongue was a hot slab of stone under her fingertips. It felt like secrets and like sex, and Sue pressed her thighs together again.

"Thank you." Sue slipped her fingers out of Kara's mouth.

"There is no reason to thank me. I wanted you. Or do you still not believe it?"

"I do believe it. But I didn't just mean for that. I meant for the song, too."

"Is it so surprising I would give you what you ask?"

"It would surprise most humans." Sue laughed. "If it didn't scare them half to death."

"That isn't what I asked."

Sue cupped Kara's chin. "You whipped my back bloody and then struck a deal with the Devil for me."

"That is so."

"And hell is a world, just past some wormhole. Fly past the ends of the galaxy and take a left."

Kara tilted her head. It reminded Sue of the alien she'd thought Kara was, all those weeks ago when she'd chased a dream through a rift.

"Kara." Sue's own voice stopped her short. Clear and strong and not quite like herself. Like she might have sounded if not for her leg, if not for the boy, if she'd become that starfighter pilot she'd wanted to be.

Kara's eyes opened wide. They flashed, a sudden flare of surprise.

Kara was impressed. Sue decided she liked it.

"Kara," she said again, in that rich tone that wasn't quite her own. "Nothing surprises me anymore." She moved her hand down Kara's neck, felt the stony roughness under her fingers.

"Is that so?" Kara chuckled.

Sue ignored it. "Not from this world and not from you."

She pulled Kara's face closer to hers, a frail little human gesture. An immortal could easily resist.

Kara didn't. She opened her mouth like she wanted to talk again. Sue stopped it with another kiss.

This wasn't home. Not for Sue and not for Kara. But they both had chosen it, all the same.

THE END

About the Author

Alexa Black lives in the Washington, DC, area, where she works as a peer mentor and advocate for people with disabilities. She was a finalist in the erotica category of the 2017 Lambda Literary Awards.

She has a master's degree in philosophy from Georgetown University, but has always returned to her passion for writing. Though a philosopher by training, she would rather inflict complicated questions on her characters and take readers along than lecture about them. When not writing, she can be found gaming, seeking out new restaurants to try, or drinking ridiculous, fancy coffee.

She can be found online at
www.facebook.com/alexablackwriter
and emailed at alexablack44@gmail.com

Books Available from Bold Strokes Books

Exposed by MJ Williamz. The closet is no place to live if you want to find true love. (978-1-62639-989-1)

Force of Fire: Toujours a Vous by Ali Vali. Immortals Kendal and Piper welcome their new child and celebrate the defeat of an old enemy, but another ancient evil is about to awaken deep in the jungles of Costa Rica. (978-1-63555-047-4)

Holding Their Place by Kelly A. Wacker. Together Dr. Helen Connery and ambulance driver Julia March, discover that goodness, love, and passion can be found in the most unlikely and even dangerous places during WWI. (978-1-63555-338-3)

Landing Zone by Erin Dutton. Can a career veteran finally discover a love stronger than even her pride? (978-1-63555-199-0)

Love at Last Call by M. Ullrich. Is balancing business, friendship, and love more than any willing woman can handle? (978-1-63555-197-6)

Pleasure Cruise by Yolanda Wallace. Spencer Collins and Amy Donovan have few things in common, but a Caribbean cruise offers both women an unexpected chance to face one of their greatest fears: falling in love. (978-1-63555-219-5)

Running Off Radar by MB Austin. Maji's plans to win Rose back are interrupted when work intrudes and duty calls her to help a SEAL team stop a Russian mobster from harvesting gold from the bottom of Sitka Sound. (978-1-63555-152-5)

Shadow of the Phoenix by Rebecca Harwell. In the final battle for the fate of Storm's Quarry, even Nadya's and Shay's powers may not be enough. (978-1-63555-181-5)

Take a Chance by D. Jackson Leigh. There's hardly a woman within fifty miles of Pine Cone that veterinarian Trip Beaumont can't charm, except for the irritating new cop, Jamie Grant, who keeps leaving parking tickets on her truck. (978-1-63555-118-1)

The Outcasts by Alexa Black. Spacebus driver Sue Jones is running from her past. When she crash-lands on a faraway world, the Outcast Kara might be her chance for redemption. (978-1-63555-242-3)

Alias by Cari Hunter. A car crash leaves a woman with no memory and no identity. Together with Detective Bronwen Pryce, she fights to uncover a truth that might just kill them both. (978-1-63555-221-8)

Death in Time by Robyn Nyx. Working in the past is hell on your future. (978-1-63555-053-5)

Hers to Protect by Nicole Disney. High school sweethearts Kaia and Adrienne will have to see past their differences and survive the vengeance of a brutal gang if they want to be together. (978-1-63555-229-4)

Of Echoes Born by 'Nathan Burgoine. A collection of queer fantasy short stories set in Canada from Lambda Literary Award finalist 'Nathan Burgoine. (978-1-63555-096-2)

Perfect Little Worlds by Clifford Mae Henderson. Lucy can't hold the secret any longer. Twenty-six years ago, her sister did the unthinkable. (978-1-63555-164-8)

Room Service by Fiona Riley. Interior designer Olivia likes stability, but when work brings footloose Savannah into her world and into a new city every month, Olivia must decide if what makes her comfortable is what makes her happy. (978-1-63555-120-4)

Sparks Like Ours by Melissa Brayden. Professional surfers Gia Malone and Elle Britton can't deny their chemistry on and off the beach. But only one can win… (978-1-63555-016-0)

Take My Hand by Missouri Vaun. River Hemsworth arrives in Georgia intent on escaping quickly, but when she crashes her Mercedes into the Clip 'n Curl, sexy Clay Cahill ends up rescuing more than her car. (978-1-63555-104-4)

The Last Time I Saw Her by Kathleen Knowles. Lane Hudson only has twelve days to win back Alison's heart. That is if she can gather the courage to try. (978-1-63555-067-2)

Wayworn Lovers by Gun Brooke. Will agoraphobic composer Giselle Bonnaire and Tierney Edwards, a wandering soul who can't remain in one place for long, trust in the passionate love destiny hands them? (978-1-62639-995-2)

Breakthrough by Kris Bryant. Falling for a sexy ranger is one thing, but is the possibility of love worth giving up the career Kennedy Wells has always dreamed of? (978-1-63555-179-2)

Certain Requirements by Elinor Zimmerman. Phoenix has always kept her love of kinky submission strictly behind the bedroom door and inside the bounds of romantic relationships, until she meets Kris Andersen. (978-1-63555-195-2)

Dark Euphoria by Ronica Black. When a high-profile case drops in Detective Maria Diaz's lap, she forges ahead only to discover this case, and her main suspect, aren't like any other. (978-1-63555-141-9)

Fore Play by Julie Cannon. Executive Leigh Marshall falls hard for Peyton Broader, her golf pro…and an ex-con. Will she risk sabotaging her career for love? (978-1-63555-102-0)

Love Came Calling by CA Popovich. Can a romantic looking for a long-term, committed relationship and a jaded cynic too busy for love conquer life's struggles and find their way to what matters most? (978-1-63555-205-8)

Outside the Law by Carsen Taite. Former sweethearts Tanner Cohen and Sydney Braswell must work together on a federal task force to see justice served, but will they choose to embrace their second chance at love? (978-1-63555-039-9)

The Princess Deception by Nell Stark. When journalist Missy Duke realizes Prince Sebastian is really his twin sister Viola in disguise, she plays along, but when sparks flare between them, will the double deception doom their fairy-tale romance? (978-1-62639-979-2)

The Smell of Rain by Cameron MacElvee. Reyha Arslan, a wise and elegant woman with a tragic past, shows Chrys that there's still beauty to embrace and reason to hope despite the world's cruelty. (978-1-63555-166-2)

The Talebearer by Sheri Lewis Wohl. Liz's visions show her the faces of the lost and the killers who took their lives. As one by one, the murdered are found, a stranger works to stop Liz before the serial killer is brought to justice. (978-1-635550-126-6)

White Wings Weeping by Lesley Davis. The world is full of discord and hatred, but how much of it is just human nature when an evil with sinister intent is invading people's hearts? (978-1-63555-191-4)

A Call Away by KC Richardson. Can a businesswoman from a big city find the answers she's looking for, and possibly love, on a small-town farm? (978-1-63555-025-2)

Berlin Hungers by Justine Saracen. Can the love between an RAF woman and the wife of a Luftwaffe pilot, former enemies, survive in besieged Berlin during the aftermath of World War II? (978-1-63555-116-7)

Blend by Georgia Beers. Lindsay and Piper are like night and day. Working together won't be easy, but not falling in love might prove the hardest job of all. (978-1-63555-189-1)

Hunger for You by Jenny Frame. Principe of an ancient vampire clan Byron Debrek must save her one true love from falling into the hands of her enemies and into the middle of a vampire war. (978-1-63555-168-6)

Mercy by Michelle Larkin. FBI Special Agent Mercy Parker and psychic ex-profiler Piper Vasey learn to love again as they race to stop a man with supernatural gifts who's bent on annihilating humankind. (978-1-63555-202-7)

Pride and Porters by Charlotte Greene. Will pride and prejudice prevent these modern-day lovers from living happily ever after? (978-1-63555-158-7)

Rocks and Stars by Sam Ledel. Kyle's struggle to own who she is and what she really wants may end up landing her on the bench and without the woman of her dreams. (978-1-63555-156-3)

The Boss of Her: Office Romance Novellas by Julie Cannon, Aurora Rey, and M. Ullrich. Going to work never felt so good. Three office romance novellas from talented writers Julie Cannon, Aurora Rey, and M. Ullrich. (978-1-63555-145-7)

The Deep End by Ellie Hart. When family ties become entangled in murder and deception, it's time to find a way out… (978-1-63555-288-1)

A Country Girl's Heart by Dena Blake. When Kat Jackson gets a second chance at love, following her heart will prove the hardest decision of all. (978-1-63555-134-1)

Dangerous Waters by Radclyffe. Life, death, and war on the home front. Two women join forces against a powerful opponent, nature itself. (978-1-63555-233-1)

Fury's Death by Brey Willows. When all we hold sacred fails, who will be there to save us? (978-1-63555-063-4)

It's Not a Date by Heather Blackmore. Kade's desire to keep things with Jen on a professional level is in Jen's best interest. Yet what's in Kade's best interest…is Jen. (978-1-63555-149-5)

Killer Winter by Kay Bigelow. Just when she thought things could get no worse, homicide Lieutenant Leah Samuels learns the woman she loves has betrayed her in devastating ways. (978-1-63555-177-8)

Score by MJ Williamz. Will an addiction to pain pills destroy Ronda's chance with the woman she loves or will she come out on top and score a happily ever after? (978-1-62639-807-8)

Spring's Wake by Aurora Rey. When wanderer Willa Lange falls for Provincetown B&B owner Nora Calhoun, will past hurts and a fifteen-year age gap keep them from finding love? (978-1-63555-035-1)

The Northwoods by Jane Hoppen. When Evelyn Bauer, disguised as her dead husband, George, travels to a Northwoods logging camp to work, she and the camp cook Sarah Bell forge a friendship fraught with both tenderness and turmoil. (978-1-63555-143-3)

Truth or Dare by C. Spencer. For a group of six lesbian friends, life changes course after one long snow-filled weekend. (978-1-63555-148-8)